D1765749

BRENT LIBRARIES

Please return/renew this item
by the last date shown.
Books may also be renewed by
phone or online.
Tel: 0333 370 4700
On-line www.brent.gov.uk/libraryservice

9112000461410

First published in this edition in Great Britain in 2020
www.francesmensahwilliams.com

Copyright ©2020 Frances Mensah Williams
Print edition published February 2021

A CIP catalogue record for this book is available from the
British Library

ISBN 978-0-9569175-8-4

Typeset by Aimee Dewar
Cover illustration by Ashley Santoro

For Akua, with love

Also by Frances Mensah Williams

Imperfect Arrangements
From Pasta to Pigfoot
From Pasta to Pigfoot: Second Helpings

Marula Heights Romance Novella Series
River Wild

Non-Fiction

Everyday Heroes: Learning from the Careers of Successful
Black Professionals
I Want to Work in Africa: How to Move Your Career to the
World's Most Exciting Continent
Enterprise Africa: A Guide to Planning Your Business in Africa

Sweetness comes at a price...

When sweet-natured Mercy married successful businessman and aspiring politician, Lucas Peterson, she abandoned her media career to focus on her husband and raising her son, Hakeem. But with the country now hurtling towards elections, Lucas's eye is on the ministerial position he craves within the Party and when Mercy's best friend, Araba – the niece of the Party leader – returns to Ghana, Mercy refuses to see what's obvious to everyone.

In a desperate bid to regain control of her life, Mercy reaches out to her friend, Max Bamford, a ruthless media boss with a reputation for uncovering corruption. Max's lifeline changes everything, but Mercy's hopes for a new beginning are threatened by Lucas's ambitions and risk the happiness of the person she loves most.

Armed with devastating evidence that can destroy Lucas's political future, Mercy is torn between protecting her son and taking revenge on his father. Faced with an impossible dilemma, Mercy will have to prove that sweetness can be a strength.

Chapter 1

The bays at the back of Swanson's were crammed with luxury cars but Mercy wasn't here to find a parking space, or even to shop at the high-end supermarket; she simply needed to see for herself if her husband's car was one of those parked in the crowded lot. Because if Lucas was in that store then Mercy knew, absolutely knew, that she – whoever she was – would be in there with him.

She slowed her car down to steer round the last row of vehicles and, seconds later, slammed her foot on the brake. There it was. Lucas had left the house less than an hour earlier to play tennis with his brother, or so he had claimed, and yet here was her husband's silver Mercedes with its unmistakable personalised number plates.

The adrenalin that had pumped through her, fuelling her anger during her drive from their home in Marula Heights into the busy town centre, drained away, leaving her feeling nauseous, dizzy and scared. Although she'd known he'd be here, she hadn't *really* known. Lucas's ridiculously late stints at the office, his sudden need to take phone calls at night in his study instead of lounging on the couch with his booming voice drowning out her favourite TV shows, his erratic interest in making love to her – all of these had been clues with only one realistic explanation. And yet, even as her unvoiced suspicions had slowly hardened into certainty, Mercy had clung to

1

the possibility she was wrong. Until today.

'I'll pick you up and we can get whatever you need from Swanson's.' Standing behind the half-open study door with Lucas oblivious to her presence, Mercy's face had prickled with heat listening to the deep-throated teasing chuckle which was usually guaranteed to make her smile. But there was nothing funny about what came next. *'You love bragging about what a great cook you are, and I can't wait to put it to the test. Something tells me your cooking will be as...* good *as everything else.'*

Mercy shook her head violently, as if the action would expel the words she had replayed countless times in her mind. She wasn't naïve. She knew important men like Lucas were constantly sought after by women looking for a protector or a benefactor or, God forbid, a sugar daddy. But she had always trusted Lucas. She *loved* him and he loved *her.* She was his sweet Mercy, wasn't that what he always said?

She jumped at the sound of an impatient honk from behind and stepped on the accelerator with more force than she'd planned, causing the tyres to screech against the tarmac. She drove around the car park again, coming to a stop behind a black Land Rover stationed alongside the far wall, its bulk fitting snugly between the thick white lines of the bay. Her chest felt as if an invisible hand had reached inside to squeeze her lungs and she loosened her grip on the steering wheel and reached into her handbag to pull out her pump. Inhaling deeply, Mercy held her breath for a long moment and willed her ragged breathing back under control. *This is not the time for an asthma attack!* She pulled up the handbrake and left the engine running while the inhaler did its work – it was far too hot to turn off the air conditioning – and flipped down the windscreen visor to shield her face from the shoppers strolling back to their cars, grimacing at the futility of the move even as she made it. This was Accra. Everyone knew everyone's business and her distinctive lilac Mazda convertible was extremely recognisable. She had lost count of the times Lucas would return home and casually mention that one of his colleagues had seen her car in town. An observation invariably followed by a charming but relentless interrogation which persisted until he was satisfied.

'You have to remember, my sweet Mercy, even the most innocent actions on your part could be misinterpreted and cost me a ministerial portfolio when the Party comes to power.'

If the Party comes to power, Mercy thought bitterly, wiping the dampness off her forehead with the back of her hand. Despite the air conditioning, the whirlwind of emotions since she'd overheard the phone call to *her*, coupled with anxiety at being caught by Lucas for spying on him – even though she wasn't the one who had done anything wrong – was causing her to sweat. She glanced at the small square mirror on the visor and frowned; without make-up, her skin looked dull and her soft brown eyes reflected her misery. She tilted her head upwards and winced as the beginnings of a double chin came into view. *Exactly when did my cheekbones disappear?* Probably around the same time as my ambition, she answered silently. She knew she was privileged to not have to work; after all, didn't Lucas remind her of that often enough?

But however she felt about her homemaker status, just trying to be a good wife and mother and keep a beautiful home her husband could be proud of took more effort than people realised. It wasn't her fault she had so little time to take care of herself and make use of the gym membership Lucas had bought her, even though he'd stressed how important it was for the wife of a future minister to look the part. Was that why he was involved with another woman? Did *she* look the part?

Mercy groaned and dropped her head onto the steering wheel, fighting the temptation to drive out of the cramped car park, pretend she had never heard those fateful words, and somehow convince herself that nothing had changed.

'*Mercy*! Is that you?'

The muffled words were followed by a sharp rap on the window and she looked up, struggling to identify through the haze of her tears the tall figure standing by her door. The man stooped and she reluctantly lowered the window, blinking hard until the face came into focus.

'Max!' Her voice was husky from the pain pressing on her chest and she cleared her throat and forced a smile.

'Sorry if I startled you. I just popped into Swanson's to pick up some sweets for my nephews. My sister will kill me, but it's the only way to make sure I remain their favourite uncle.' He chuckled, and then nodded towards the Range Rover she had blocked in. 'You can have my parking space if you're going inside?'

'No!' The word came out more sharply than she had intended, and she immediately regretted it when his brows knotted in concern. Max Bamford was like a

Rottweiler when it came to pouncing on the unwary. Which was probably what made him such a brilliant journalist and interviewer, she thought ruefully. It was common knowledge that the high-profile guests who appeared on *The Bamford Report* were torn between the kudos of being seen on the highly rated public affairs TV show and their fear of being picked apart by Max's disarming and surgically incisive style of questioning. Even Lucas, desperate as he was to raise his profile within the Party, had resisted Max's persistent invitations to appear on the show. Despite Mercy and Max's long friendship, her husband had yet to be persuaded to take his chances in the infamous black armchair.

'Are you okay?' Max's frown hadn't shifted, and she attempted a smile.

'Yes, of course. It's just – well, you know... hot, that's all.' Her foot tapped nervously on the accelerator.

'How's Lucas getting on?' Max appeared to be in no hurry to end the conversation.

Mercy released a slow breath. Clearly, he hadn't spotted her husband in the supermarket with *her*. She shrugged and tried to keep her voice even.

'Fine. You know... busy with the Party, as usual. We hardly see him these days, what with the elections only a couple of months away. You know how it is, all the Party members are out campaigning morning, noon and night.' *Or at least that's the excuse he gives us.*

'And Hakeem?'

At the sound of her beloved son's name, Mercy's forced smile was instantly transformed into a genuine grin. 'He's great! He finally got picked for the junior football team at school and he scored the winning goal during his first match last weekend.' *And his father didn't turn up as promised because he was probably with his mistress.*

Suddenly conscious that if Lucas came out with *her* and Max saw them, he would put two and two together, Mercy added quickly, 'You know what, I *do* need to buy some cheese. They have a great selection here, don't they? Not that it's cheap – I mean, it's ridiculous the amount of money you have to spend just for...' she tailed off as she ran out of words. 'I'll move so you can reverse out,' she concluded lamely.

Max hesitated, his dark eyes probing hers for a few moments, and then he nodded and straightened up. He pushed the paper bag he had been holding into one pocket and rummaged in the other for a silver key fob.

'It's good to see you, Mercy,' he said softly. 'I can't remember the last time we sat down and talked properly. I know Lucas isn't exactly a fan of mine, but it would be nice to see more of you.'

Forgetting for a moment that she was hiding in a car park trying to catch her husband with his mistress, Mercy's lips widened into a smile. 'I don't think there's a single politician in this country who's a fan of yours. After that exposé you broke on the Minister – or rather the ex-Minister – you have them all trembling in their shoes.'

Max gave a rueful shrug. 'Trust me, it doesn't give me any pleasure to ruin people's lives. But we're a young democracy with a fragile economy, and I'm not giving anyone who tries to rip this country off a pass. If there's nothing to hide, there's no reason for anyone to fear me.'

He smiled. 'I'd better get these sweets to the boys before they melt in my pocket.'

He made as if to walk away, and then stopped and turned back to eye her squarely. 'When are you going to get bored of playing the politician's wife and come and join my team? Sigh all you want, but I'm not going to stop asking. Look, Mercy, in university you were one of the best writers in our year, and you could still have a fantastic career in media. I need a new staff writer on my production team   would you at least think about it?'

She darted a glance towards the supermarket's exit doors and then returned her gaze to Max. Her gaze took in his casual chinos and dark brown loafers and she ruthlessly suppressed the tiny flutter of longing brought on by the broad shoulders and muscular arms which his loose white shirt couldn't quite disguise.

'Max, I've told you before. I'm flattered, but—'

'I know, I know. You're busy looking after Lucas. But does that mean you have to stop looking after yourself?'

Mercy smiled up at him. 'Even after all these years, you're still so protective of me.'

'I think we both know that protective doesn't describe how I feel about you.'

'*Max!*'

'Don't worry, I'm a big boy. And a professional, so you've nothing to worry about if you decide to work with me,' he added with a wry grin. 'Just think about it, that's all I ask.'

Mercy's smile faded. It *was* good to see him, but this wasn't the time to keep Max talking or to entertain even the mildest flirtation. Besides all of that – *that* with Max, whatever she imagined it had been or, indeed, could have been – was firmly in the past. She murmured something non-committal and pointedly put her car into gear. A momentary hesitation on his part was followed by a nod of farewell before he strode to his car and leaped in. Seconds later, he expertly reversed out of the tight spot and drove off.

Mercy backed into the space and then inched her car forward so she could see the sliding doors used by shoppers to enter the car park. She reluctantly turned off the engine and lowered the windows to let in some fresh air, and within moments the intense heat from the afternoon sun was beating mercilessly through the open window, accompanied by a foul smell emanating from several overflowing waste bins a few metres away. She was tempted to drive around again, but she couldn't risk Lucas seeing her. And besides, she had no intention of moving until she saw *her*. The woman who had managed somehow to seduce her loving husband.

Mercy's eyes welled up at the thought of Lucas together with another woman and she bit down hard on her tongue to stop herself wailing with the same wild abandon as the women hired to weep at funerals. This wasn't the place to make a scene – God forbid, what if one of Hakeem's friends' parents saw her, just as Max had done? She would rather die in silence than risk having her son's friends laugh at him because his mother had gone mad in the car park at Swanson's!

She desperately wished she could call Araba. She had never felt more in need of her best friend, and her hand inched towards the phone on the seat beside her before reluctantly creeping back into her lap. She felt far too fragile to deal with the drama that telling Araba would undoubtedly provoke. Where Mercy was naturally diffident and accommodating of others, Araba had never been anything other than bold and uncompromising. To most people, the two women were the unlikeliest of friends, but Mercy and Araba had been inseparable since their first day at university when they had been randomly paired to share a room in halls. Neither spared the other their secrets and so, just as Mercy learned how badly Araba wanted to join her mother in the UK after graduation and make her name as a top lawyer, Araba became the confidante who understood Mercy's deep longing to fall in love, get married and have a home bursting with children. Having grown up with a depressive mother who rarely left her bed, and a largely absent father who left her in the charge of a series of aunties during school holidays, Mercy's childhood had been an intensely lonely experience. Unlike the other girls at her boarding school who couldn't wait for the holidays so they could attend parties and social get-togethers, or even travel abroad, school had offered Mercy a refuge from her oppressively silent house and the parade of indifferent relatives and maids who cared only about her material needs. At university, Araba had quickly filled the emotional void by becoming the sister Mercy had never had, immediately taking charge of her and subsequently making decisions for them both. 'You're too sweet for your own good, Mercy, you need to toughen up!' was a frequent complaint. Mercy, intensely grateful for her new friend, had had no trouble overlooking Araba's fiery nature and fierce over-protectiveness.

Araba had been especially zealous in guarding Mercy from the distractions posed by the men eager to ask out her famously sweet-natured friend. For three years, Araba had stymied the efforts of anyone whom she deemed unworthy or who, in her view, was pursuing Mercy solely to take advantage of her. Consequently, it was only because Araba had decamped to London by the time Lucas appeared on the scene a couple of years after graduation that Mercy's relationship with Lucas had been allowed to flourish unhindered. From the start, Lucas's sophistication and charm had won Mercy over, quickly banishing any doubts on her part about the ten-year age gap between them. Unlike the boys of her own age, Lucas was a grown-up, and a man who was clearly ready to make a commitment. Before long they became an established couple and when Lucas proposed after only seven months together, Mercy had accepted without hesitation. Hakeem was born twelve months later, and Mercy's reluctance to leave him with a nanny at the end of her maternity leave had spurred Lucas to insist that she resign her media job and enjoy being a full-time wife and mother. But having given up her career for her dream of a big family, Mercy had been unable to fall pregnant since her son's birth. To her deep frustration and sadness, despite the battery of tests revealing no problem with either her or Lucas's fertility, Hakeem had remained an only child.

But that was then. Now, as she sat in her stiflingly hot car trying not to inhale too deeply in case the pungent fumes from the open bins triggered her asthma, Mercy drummed on the steering wheel and chewed her lower lip miserably. One of the unwritten rules of her friendship with Araba was that they were completely honest with each other, and yet she had kept Araba in the dark about her suspicions. And if she were to call Araba now to confess Lucas's transgressions, Mercy knew there would be no turning back. While twelve years in London, including a stint with a leading law firm, had turned Araba into a highly sought-after legal talent, it certainly hadn't tamed her legendary temper, and it wasn't hard to imagine how her friend would respond to Mercy's current dilemma; an impatient snort, followed by 'Mercy, what is *wrong* with you? Wait there and I'll come over and rip the bitch's weave out!'

Mercy sighed, wishing, not for the first time, that she could be more like her best friend. There was no way Araba would be skulking out here in the shadows. Knowing her, she'd have marched into Swanson's like a hungry lion in search of her prey and torn *her* limb from limb before boldly confronting Lucas – more than likely slapping him in full view of everyone before telling him in no uncertain terms where to go.

Mercy shuddered. No, she couldn't do that to her husband. However bad his behaviour, he had an important job and Ghana needed smart, honest politicians like him. *Honest? Really, Mercy?* Suddenly, she couldn't hold back the sobs that broke through her tightly clenched lips and she let the pain, made so much worse by her own indecisiveness, wash over her. *Dammit, Mercy! Why the hell are you so bloody weak?*

After a few moments, she swiped at her cheeks and forced herself to gulp down the tears. She needed to hold

11

it together and keep her eyes open if she was to spot *her*. What was she like, Mercy wondered? This woman who had turned Lucas into the cheating husband she had never imagined he could be. Was she beautiful? Slim? She sat up in her seat and smoothed her skirt down over her soft thighs. Lucas always protested when she described herself as fat.

'You're not fat, my sweet Mercy. You're curvy and delicious. You have gorgeous breasts and a lush bottom. You're what every red-blooded man wants in his woman.'

Well, if I'm so delicious, what am I doing sitting out here waiting for you and your mistress? The thought flittered through her mind and then froze when she saw him striding out of the store, a bulging shopping bag in one hand and his keys dangling from the other. *So much for playing tennis with your brother, you liar!* There was no danger of Lucas spotting her, Mercy thought despairingly. His attention was completely focused on the woman walking beside him. She watched her husband throw his head back in unrestrained laughter, and icy shivers traced their way down her spine as she watched *her,* partly hidden by Lucas's broad frame, stop for a moment to lovingly stroke his face.

She was nearly as tall as Lucas and her fitted white dress displayed a lithe figure which was slimmer than Mercy could ever hope to be. *She* was carrying a smart blue bag and her long braids swung from side to side as she stalked in her towering high heels ahead of Lucas and towards the car with all the confidence of a supermodel.

She was also Mercy's best friend.

Chapter 2

The pillow was soaked from her tears and Mercy sat up and flipped it over, plucking a tissue from the box on the bedside table and blowing her nose hard. *Come on, Mercy! You've got to pull yourself together before Hakeem comes home and sees you like this.*

The last thing she wanted was for her son to burst in and find her sobbing like a child over a broken doll. She hadn't forgotten the profound anxiety she'd seen in his eyes once when she'd been unable to get out of bed after suffering a crippling migraine. No, Hakeem didn't deserve to be made unhappy because of his father's behaviour. She was the adult, and it was up to her to solve her problems without upsetting their child.

She glanced at her watch and sighed. Her son was due back at five o'clock, which gave her less than half an hour to try and at least look normal, even if her heart felt like someone had used a steel grater on it. Her mother-in-law was a stickler for punctuality, and Mercy knew she would be at their gate with her grandson at the stroke of five.

She scrambled off the bed and hurried into the en-suite bathroom where despite her best efforts, each time she rinsed her face, fresh tears would form and cascade down her cheeks. After the third attempt, she took a deep breath and looked up at the ceiling, forcing herself to picture Hakeem's face. After a moment, she lowered her head and although her eyes remained moist, this time she managed to hold the tears at bay. When it came to her son, she could find the strength to do almost anything. Araba often teased that despite her sweet nature, Mercy was like a mother lion who would cheerfully slaughter anyone who tried to hurt Hakeem.

Araba. Just thinking about her supposed best friend almost undid Mercy's no tears resolution, and she blinked hard and clutched on to the hand basin. Just how many of the tears she had shed on her drive back to Marula Heights were the product of Lucas's betrayal and how many were because of Araba was hard to tell. Yes, Lucas was her husband and she loved him, but he was also a product of his society where, if she was brutally honest, an unfaithful husband was too often seen as par for the course. Araba, however, was her sister – or as good as – and there was nothing in the world that made it okay for her to have an affair with her husband. Even now, the scale of Araba's betrayal was simply too hard to comprehend.

In that moment, for the first time since meeting Araba, Mercy felt stinging, bitter resentment at the woman she had loved sweep through her in a torrent of bile. She had trusted Araba too much to ever question her behaviour, ignoring what had clearly been well-meaning advice from Stella, who had been her best friend before Araba had re-entered her life, and from her mother-in-law, both of whom considered Araba to be over-familiar in her dealings with Mercy's domestic staff and, yes, her husband. Why had she never noticed how often Araba would find excuses to come over in the evenings when Lucas was at home? Why hadn't she seen through her friend's frequent probing questions about Mercy's marriage and the warnings Araba had issued more than once, albeit accompanied each time by a teasing laugh, that as the niece of the Party Chairman, Lucas would have to stay in her good graces to progress. Was this what it was all about for Lucas, Mercy mused? Did he want to be a minister so badly that he was prepared to risk their marriage?

A surge of uncontrollable fury propelled Mercy back into the bedroom. She snatched her phone off the bedside table and without stopping to think, she punched Araba's number and then gripped the handset so tightly her knuckles ached. The call was answered almost immediately.

'Hey, girl! What's up?' Araba sounded cheerful enough, but to Mercy's suspicious ears, there was a tinge of wariness hovering just beneath the words.

'Nothing much,' Mercy replied, trying to keep her voice even while her chest threatened to burst with misery. 'I went into town earlier. I just got back.'

'Oh, yes?' Was there a slight note of hesitancy there, Mercy wondered?

'Yes. I needed some groceries and Hakeem wanted me to get him a packet of those American sweets they sell at Swanson's – the chewy ones he and Jamie are so obsessed with.'

This time, Mercy didn't imagine the pause that followed.

'And?'

'And what?'

'And did you get them – the sweets?'

This time it was Mercy's turn to hesitate. *I'm not ready to do this yet. I can't!*

'No, there was too much traffic in Osu. I decided to leave it until tomorrow.'

Araba was silent for a moment. 'Sounds like you did the right thing. I still can't get over how much traffic there is in town these days. I thought London was bad, but at least there's a good public transport system over there.'

Angry at herself for pretending, and yet knowing she didn't want a showdown with Araba on the phone, Mercy was relieved when the sound of a car horn wafted through the bedroom window. Even though Marula Heights was a secure gated estate, the larger houses were walled for additional security and guarded by a watchman who sat inside the front gates.

'I'd better go. Lucas's mother is here with Hakeem.' Without waiting for a reply, Mercy cut off the call, her finger trembling from the effort of holding her emotions in check. She inhaled deeply and released a shaky breath before heading downstairs to open the front door.

'Mummy, look what Grandma gave me!' Hakeem rushed in with such speed to hug her that he nearly knocked Mercy off balance. She held on to him for a moment to steady herself and despite her inner turmoil, she couldn't help laughing at the excitement in his seven-year-old eyes.

'Calm down, Hakeem! You can show me in a minute. Let me greet Grandma first,' she chided gently. She gave the box in his hand a fleeting glance before steering him to one side and moving forward to greet her mother-in-law.

'Good afternoon, Mama. You are welcome – please come in.'

Lucas's mother was nearly as tall as her son and towered over Mercy's five feet and two inches. Dressed in a flowing black and blue patterned traditional gown, the older lady graciously inclined a head of short, white natural curls.

'Good afternoon, Mercy.'

After offering Mercy her cheek for a kiss, the older woman took the lead and Mercy followed her into the spacious living room and watched her settle herself into an armchair. She bit back a smile as her mother-in-law carefully placed her handbag on the side table. In all the years she'd known her, Mercy couldn't remember ever seeing her without the accessory, even when she was relaxing in her own home. 'You'd think she was Queen Elizabeth the way she always has a handbag dangling from her elbow,' was Lucas's frequent exasperated complaint.

'May I bring you something to drink, Mama?'

Disregarding the question, the woman beckoned to her to come closer. Her eyes zeroed in on Mercy's face and she spoke softly, 'My daughter, have you been crying?'

But before Mercy could answer, Hakeem dashed into the room and pulled excitedly on her arm, holding up a large, metallic blue robot. 'Mummy, *look*! Grandma said it's an early Christmas present.'

'*Christmas*? But we're still in October, Mama!'

Hakeem's grandmother shrugged. 'There was a sale at the toy shop in the mall and I didn't see any point waiting for two months to buy the same thing at twice the price. Hakeem,' she turned to the boy and gave him a conspiratorial wink, 'why don't you take the toy to your room before Mummy decides to keep it wrapped until Christmas?'

With a panicked expression, Hakeem sped out of the room and Lucas's mother turned her attention back to Mercy. 'Sit down, my dear.'

Mercy cleared her throat nervously. Her mother-in-law had been a lawyer until her retirement, and she hadn't yet lost her ability to interrogate the unwary.

'Tell me, my daughter. What has made you, of all people, unhappy?'

Mercy shook her head, the gentle words immediately setting off a prickling behind her eyes. She was tempted to pour out her anguish but her mother-in-law, as kind as she was, was first and foremost Lucas's mother.

'It – it's nothing, Mama. I was just feeling a little low, that's all.'

'That doesn't sound like you,' came the sceptical rejoinder. 'Quite frankly, my dear, you have the most endearing and irritating capacity to *not* feel low. And yet, instead of your usual sweet smile, your eyes look like those of a sad puppy. Has Lucas upset you?'

'N–no, Mama. Of course not!' Mercy protested. *I can't tell her the truth. Not yet.*

She quickly added, 'Besides, he's hardly ever at home to be able to upset me. He's always out campaigning, and with the elections—'

'If it's his absence that's the problem, Mercy, then you must forgive him. These elections will be one of the most critical ever for our country, and we must all be prepared to sacrifice to see the Party succeed. This country has been through such turmoil – if the Party is elected, they will change so many things for the better.'

Grateful that she was no longer the subject of the conversation, Mercy held her tongue while her mother-in-law enthused about how the Party's published manifesto would surely return Ghana to the path of prosperity from which previous misguided governments had caused it to stray.

'... and once Lucas secures a ministerial post, he is so popular that the next step will surely be the vice presidency. I know my son, and I'm convinced he'll be able to bring about the change we desperately need to see. You know better than anyone how determined he is to introduce new policies to reduce poverty and improve all our lives. And, just imagine, Mercy, if all goes well and the Party wins yet another term, the old man has made it clear he'll step aside as leader – which means Lucas could well become the President!'

Having just learned to her cost exactly how determined Lucas was to secure his position in the Party, Mercy smiled weakly and tried to muster some enthusiasm before she replied. 'Yes, Mama. Imagine...'

* * *

An hour later, with her son by her side, Mercy waved goodbye to her mother-in-law and watched her drive away. Relieved to be able to drop the cheery façade she had maintained for Lucas's mother, Mercy sent the boy inside to wash his hands and tidy his bedroom while she walked slowly back into the house. Hakeem's trophy from his first football match sat on the table in the hallway and she picked it up and took it through to Lucas's study. As Lucas hadn't been at the sidelines to watch his son's triumph, Mercy thought, she could at least make sure the trophy took pride of place in the room where Lucas was most often to be found these days. However she felt about her husband's behaviour, she knew Hakeem adored his father and would be thrilled by the gesture.

Mercy stood in the doorway for a moment, reliving the conversation she had unwittingly eavesdropped upon. It felt like days rather than mere hours since she'd overheard Lucas's flirtatious conversation, and she switched on the light to brighten the gloom of the room and in her heart.

The study was in a state of near chaos and smelled a little musty from the newspapers piled onto every conceivable surface. The huge desk was covered with paper files and dominated by a desktop computer with double monitors, and two heavy bookcases bracketing the desk were filled to overflowing with books ranging from political biographies to Lucas's favourite thrillers. With no space left on the crammed bookshelves, the stacks of books piled on the floor behind the desk reminded Mercy that she needed to arrange for another bookcase to be installed.

She looked around with a sigh. The room could use a good clean, but Lucas had banned the house help from entering, refusing to take the risk of his staff being bribed to leak confidential Party communiques to the press. Carefully navigating her way through the piles of newspapers on the thick rug covering the parquet flooring, Mercy cleared a space on a bookshelf for the award and then stepped back to check the trophy would be visible from behind the desk. Satisfied, she turned to go, and her leg bumped against an open desk drawer. She winced and then stooped to pull out a manila file that had wedged itself into the corner of the drawer, preventing it from closing. Flipping open the folder to straighten the papers that had been shoved inside in some haste and with their corners sticking out untidily, she absently scanned the first few words on the top sheet and her hands stilled. She took in the neatly typed words and the columns of figures and, instinctively, her fingers moved to cover her mouth as she read on, horrified at the level of detail in the information set out. She laid the folder on the desk and flipped through the remaining sheets, her heart racing faster with each one she turned over. The only other item in the folder was a small envelope and her fingers trembled as she slowly slid the unsealed flap open and eased out the contents. It took her a moment to register what the three photographs revealed, and she sank onto the desk before her legs gave way. *What the hell! How could she have lived with this man, loved this man, and not known he was capable of this?*

The sound of the gate creaking open jolted Mercy out of her reverie. *Lucas!* The study was at the front of the house and she could hear the powerful engine of his Mercedes as it powered up and around the driveway to park under the corrugated iron roof of the carport. She scrabbled furiously in her pocket for her phone, and her fingers trembled as she trained her camera on to the papers in the file. She heard the car door slam and clicked away furiously.

21

'Mercy! Where are you?' She snapped the last photograph and shoved the folder back into the desk drawer just as Lucas's voice carried into the study from the hallway. Nudging the drawer shut with her knee, Mercy moved swiftly across to the bookcase and was making a show of straightening the trophy when he strode in.

'Why didn't you answer me? What are you doing in here?' he asked, his voice suddenly sharper than it had sounded seconds earlier.

Mercy stared at him for a moment, her eyes taking in the short-sleeved linen shirt that skimmed his toned physique, and his immaculately pressed trousers. There was no streak of the deep red lipstick Araba favoured on his white shirt and she fleetingly wondered if she was imagining things and that Lucas wasn't an unfaithful monster.

'Hakeem asked me to put his football trophy where you'd see it when you were working,' she lied smoothly. *Two can play that game, can't they?*

The look of suspicion was immediately transformed into one of guilt-tinged ruefulness. 'Of course. I'm sorry I had to miss the match, but—'

'But you had to travel on Party business,' she finished, unable to help the sarcastic tone that coated her words. Lucas's expression darkened, and his brows knitted together in almost comical puzzlement. He's certainly not accustomed to his sweet Mercy challenging his version of events, she thought viciously.

'Is there something wrong, Mercy?'

'I don't know, Lucas. Is there?' Despite her bravado,

22

her voice caught in her throat and her eyes teared up again. She cursed herself silently for showing weakness when she wanted to leap on him and tear his eyes out like a crazed lioness... just like Araba would have. But then, as she reminded herself sadly, she wasn't Araba, and wasn't *that* the problem?

Seeing her eyes well up, Lucas exclaimed and moved towards her, but furious at herself as much as at him, she raised a hand to ward him off.

'Don't – don't touch me!'

He stopped in his tracks and narrowed his eyes. 'Mercy, what the hell is going on? Why are you behaving this way? If you're feeling unwell, you need to pull yourself together. This is not the time for you to start falling apart. I don't need to remind you that with the elections coming up—'

'If I hear that word *one* more time, I swear I will scream!' Mercy ground out furiously. She advanced towards her husband who was now staring at her with undisguised astonishment. 'Don't talk to me about the importance of keeping up appearances when you are sleeping with my *friend*!'

Lucas blinked rapidly as the import of her words struck home. She watched a succession of expressions cross his face: first incredulity, then panic, followed by wariness, and finally Lucas's default expression – arrogance.

'You're talking nonsense, Mercy,' he said calmly. 'I don't know what's put that idea into your head. I'm your husband. You know me, and you know I wouldn't do any such thing. And neither would Araba.'

'I said my friend – I didn't mention Araba's name.'

His eyes shifted away from hers. 'Well, I just assumed...' he tailed off with a shrug. 'In any case, whatever you're imagining is simply not true. You know Araba thinks of you as her sister.'

'Oh, did she tell you that when you were together? And when was that, Lucas? When did you last see her?' Mercy challenged, her eyes drilling into him.

'I don't know exactly... wasn't she here a couple of days ago?' His tone suddenly shifted from defensive to deeply offended. 'Mercy, I honestly don't know what's got into you and why you are making such a wild accusation. It's very hurtful. I'm trying my best to be a good husband and father and with the elec— um, at this point, I need your full support.'

Suddenly, it was all too much for Mercy. First, Araba's shocking betrayal, then the awful contents of the manila folder, and now Lucas, the man she trusted – *had* trusted – with her life, was blatantly lying to her.

'You're a liar, Lucas! A *liar*!' she screamed, the rawness of her pain ripping away any vestige of calmness.

Lucas slammed the study door shut and turned to face her, his back against the door as if for support. 'Mercy, for God's sake, keep your voice down! Hakeem is in the house!'

'Is *that* all you're concerned about?' Mercy wailed. 'That your son will hear me and know that his father is a liar and a cheat? That's right, Lucas, a *cheat*!'

The nonplussed expression on his face acted like fuel gushing onto a raging fire. 'Don't take me for a fool. I *heard* you, Lucas, and I *saw* you and *her*! I saw you together...

I *saw* you!' Her voice broke and she fell to her knees, sobbing so hard she didn't notice him approach until she felt his hand rest tentatively on her shoulder.

'Mercy, *please*! It's not what you think. It— I... please stop crying. I wouldn't do that to you. You're my sweet Mercy. Please, get up, come *on*...'

She wailed even louder. 'Don't you dare deny it! Don't try and make out that I'm some crazy woman who can't see what's going on in front of her own eyes.'

For a long moment there was silence. When she eventually raised her head, Lucas was staring down at her thoughtfully. Then he shrugged. 'Well, you obviously *didn't* see what was going on, did you, Mercy?'

She gasped, but he paid no attention to her stunned expression and continued in a tone as casual as if he was discussing the weather. 'You're right, there's no point denying it — and I suppose even you would have figured it out sooner or later. Yes, I admit I've been seeing Araba, but I'm afraid you're going to have to come to terms with that.'

'*Lucas*! You don't mean that.' Too shocked to continue crying, she stared up at him open-mouthed.

'Look, Mercy, I'm sorry. I honestly didn't want you to find out this way – or at all, if I'm honest. It really wasn't my intention to hurt you but... maybe now you know, it's no bad thing. We just have to be adults about this— well, you know, this... situation.'

Mercy stumbled to her feet and backed away from him until she felt the solidity of the desk behind her. She felt like she'd inadvertently stumbled into a surreal nightmare and prayed she would wake up to find her life hadn't been turned upside down and her loving husband wasn't an unfeeling brute.

With the self-satisfied assurance of one who had successfully resolved a problem, Lucas walked past her and picked up a couple of sealed envelopes lying on his desk. He slit them both open with a steel letter opener and tossed the sharp dagger onto his desk. For a brief second, Mercy fought the impulse to seize the blade and stab it through her husband's lying heart. Then she thought of Hakeem and sagged helplessly onto the corner of the desk.

'Lucas, you have to stop seeing her.' She heard the naked plea in her voice – and despised herself for it. But Hakeem worshipped his father, and if she had to beg to keep her son from finding out the truth about him, she would do it. 'I'll forgive you, but you have to promise me you'll stop seeing her.'

Lucas looked up from the letter he'd been perusing and shot her a look of incredulity. 'Do you think you are in any position to tell me what to do or who I can and can't see?'

'Lucas, you're my *husband*!'

'Yes, and haven't I been a good husband to you? Look around you – how many women are lucky enough to live in a house like this? You don't even have to go out to work. Really, Mercy, have you ever stopped to consider how lucky you are?'

'*Lucky*!' She echoed in disbelief, infuriated by his habit of rewriting history. 'I *want* to work. *You're* the one who won't let me! Every time I've mentioned resuming my career now Hakeem's started school, you've thrown up objections and made it sound like me going back to work wouldn't be fair on him.'

Lucas sighed and dropped the loose sheet onto the desk. 'Sweet, sweet Mercy, let's not fight. I know you're feeling upset right now, but you are my wife and we have a good life together. What matters now is that we continue to show the country what a happy, loving couple we are. Once the Party's in power, we'll have an even better life. My relationship with Araba isn't the end of the world. You'll see,' he added with a shrug.

'My God, Lucas, what's happened to you? Is the Party all you care about?' she marvelled. 'Are you so ambitious that you've lost all common sense? Do you honestly think the Chairman is going to approve of you cheating on your wife with his own niece? What do you think will happen if this gets out – I mean, who will want to appoint a minister who's caused a scandal before he's even in office?'

Lucas's eyes were suddenly as hard as granite. 'First of all, it *isn't* getting out. This is our business and no one else's. Secondly, you know as well as I do that the Chairman adores Araba. Who do you think paid for her education and helped her get settled in London? Trust me, he'll do anything to keep his sister and her daughter happy.'

Mercy stared at him in disbelief. Lucas really thought he could get away with treating her like this. How much contempt must he feel to disregard her as a risk to his ambitions? Her mind flipped to the information she had stumbled upon only minutes earlier, and incensed at being dismissed so easily, she raised her chin defiantly. 'I'm not stupid, Lucas. I've warned you not to take me for a fool. There are things I know...'

'What things, Mercy?'

She hesitated, torn between revealing she knew about the contents of the folder and her sudden fear at the menacing glare he was directing at her. When she didn't answer, he shook his head as if she were a naughty child he had caught out lying.

'I thought so. Whatever you think you know or don't know, my sweet Mercy, you will keep your mouth shut. Because I promise you that if you force me into a corner, you'll regret it. I know every judge in this town and if I'm pushed into having to divorce you, I guarantee I will get custody of our son. Without me, you have no job and no home, so listen carefully. Whether you want to hear it or not, we have an election to fight, and *you* will do nothing to jeopardise the Party's image. You should know by now, Mercy – I will do whatever it takes to win.'

And with that, he left the room without a backward glance.

Chapter 3

'So, how long has it been going on?'

Mercy's words remained suspended in the tense silence until Araba sighed deeply and dropped her gaze. It had taken three days before she'd rightly concluded that Mercy would continue bombarding her with phone calls until she answered. For Mercy, each passing day since the showdown with Lucas had brought a little less sadness and considerably more anger, an emotion further stoked by Araba's ongoing attempts to avoid her. Knowing Lucas would have warned his mistress that the cat was out of the bag had left Mercy fuming. How *dare* Araba think she could avoid having to account for herself?

And yet when her friend had finally answered her phone, sounding subdued instead of triumphant, Mercy had inexplicably felt her own righteous fury seep away. 'You know why I'm calling and, no, I don't want to do this on the phone. Come over. Now!'

'Now' had been an hour later, and the two women stood facing each other across the expanse of Mercy's spacious living room. Mercy felt her anger resurge and she struggled to control the overwhelming urge to leap on the other woman and rip her to shreds.

Araba sighed. 'Look, let's sit down, okay.' Without waiting for an answer, she crossed the floor to sit in the armchair next to the squashy, L-shaped sofa that dominated the room. She settled back in her chair and crossed her legs, her tight jeans emphasising their toned slimness. Immediately feeling inadequate, Mercy swallowed hard and after a moment's hesitation, she followed and perched on the edge of the sofa, facing Araba squarely.

'I asked you a question. How long have you been sleeping with my husband?'

Araba flinched but didn't immediately reply, keeping her eyes fixed on the thick patterned rug under her feet. When she finally looked up, her almond-shaped eyes, elongated by the heavy eye pencil she favoured, held Mercy's gaze with an almost hypnotic intensity. After a moment, Araba shrugged, the gesture immediately breaking the spell.

'Mercy, I understand you're angry, but—'

'*But*? Oh, there's a "but"?'

'You asked me a question and I'm trying to answer you.'

'So then answer me. How. Long. Have. You. Been. Sleeping. With. My. Husband? See, it's easy, *answer me!*'

Once again Araba dropped her gaze and her jaw set into the stubborn expression Mercy knew only too well. 'We're not just sleeping together,' she muttered.

'Excuse me?'

'I said, we're not just—' Araba broke off and took a deep breath. 'I don't want to hurt you, Mercy, but it's not just... you know, sex. I – we – really care about each other. I felt it from the first time we met, and Lucas... well, Lucas feels the same way.' She looked directly at Mercy. 'You know I wouldn't risk our friendship if it wasn't serious. We didn't plan this – honestly. We, well, we just clicked.'

Mercy listened in disbelief. 'What the *hell*, Araba! Do you hear yourself? That's my *husband* you're talking about. Where do you get the nerve to come into my home and—?'

Araba uncrossed her legs and jumped to her feet. 'You *made* me come here, remember? I didn't even want to talk to you until you'd had time to calm down and see sense.'

'*Calm down!*' Mercy spat out the words and stood up to face her. '*I* should calm down? My God, the pair of you *disgust* me! I thought I knew you, but I don't recognise what you've become.'

Clearly stung, Araba's lips tightened and her eyes blazed scorn. 'Is that so? Then you're not the only one, because I don't recognise what *you've* become. When I left Ghana, you were on a fast track to a top-flight career in the media, and now look at you! Tell me, Mercy, if *I'm* the one who's such a disappointment, what exactly was the point of you getting a degree and going through all that education just to sit in this big house and instruct Esi what to cook for dinner every day? All you ever talk about is what Hakeem did in school or – or some piece of furniture you want to buy. What the hell happened to *you*? We're months away from an election that could bring your husband to power, and all you care about is whether Lucas is coming to a kid's football match? It's no damned wonder he's bored *sick* of you!'

Stunned by the vicious onslaught, Mercy gripped the back of the sofa to steady herself. Araba's sharp cheekbones and full lips merged into a brown blur as Mercy's eyes flooded with tears.

After a moment Araba sighed, now sounding almost

31

kindly. 'My sister, please don't make me say nasty things to you. You're so sweet that it hurts me to upset you, but let's be honest. You *were* brilliant, Mercy, and you've just wasted all your talent. I tried so hard at university to protect you from men who could distract you from fulfilling your potential but looking at you now maybe I shouldn't have bothered.'

'This is *not* about me,' Mercy countered fiercely, deeply shaken by Araba's harsh accusations which, despite herself, had found an echo deep inside her own consciousness. 'It's about you and what you've been doing behind my back. What happened to us always being honest with each other?'

As if Mercy hadn't spoken, Araba continued. 'You have an excellent brain but what are you using it for? Where's your self-respect, hmm? Your son has his own friends; he doesn't need you hanging around him the whole time. Do you want him to look at you in ten years' time in the same way Lucas does now?'

Mercy hunched over as if to shield herself from the savage tirade, but the other woman hadn't finished. 'But then, why am I surprised? I mean, let's face it, if we're being *honest*,' she stressed the word mockingly, 'it's not like you were ever ambitious, is it? With you, it was always about marriage and babies. Don't get me wrong – after growing up with your crazy mother, I understood how badly you wanted a family. But if you'd met Lucas before I left for London, I would have told you that he'd never be the right man for you.'

Gasping at Araba's casual cruelty, Mercy was too shocked to speak. Apparently emboldened by the silence,

Araba nodded thoughtfully. 'Since you love your family, I hope you'll be reasonable about this. Like Lucas says, now you know what's going on, we can all come to a discreet and sensible arrangement where everyone gets what they want. With the upcoming elections—'

'*Oh my God*! Is that all you people think about? Is winning power your justification for everything?'

In her spiky heels, Araba towered over Mercy as she stepped forward to stand right in front of her. 'And that's *exactly* why you're the wrong woman for Lucas. How do you think anything gets done in this world without power? My uncle has worked for years to build the Party, and now it's ahead in the polls, he will win this election and set our country on the right road at last.'

Mercy shook her head. 'What's the point of power if you have no values, Araba? If you can betray a sister, and Lucas can betray his wife and child, what will stop you from betraying the country if you get your way?'

Araba tossed back her braids with a disbelieving laugh. 'Honestly, Mercy, you're so naïve sometimes, it's hilarious. Values don't feed people or create wealth. Making our country great isn't about *values*, it's about negotiating deals and creating policies to help put us on the map. Why do you think I left my career in London to come back home? Right now, we're practically giving away our national assets – our gold, oil and minerals are all undervalued on world markets. It's people like me who know how to negotiate with Westerners in a language they'll understand who'll be changing lives here. You'll see – once my uncle is in charge, he's going to lead us on a new path to prosperity.'

Mercy stared in wonder at Araba, both appalled and unnerved by the passion behind her narcissism and unwavering conviction. Just like Lucas. *My God, it's like they're in a cult*, she thought.

Despite herself, Mercy shivered as Lucas's words reverberated loudly around her head. *I will do whatever it takes to win.*

* * *

'Mercy!'

At the sound of the familiar voice, Mercy spun round to face the attractive, dark-skinned woman grinning at her. It had been almost a week since her bruising encounter with Araba, and much too raw to face anyone, Mercy had remained closeted at home until forced to attend Hakeem's football game. But even without her son's pleas that she come and watch him play, the choice had been stark: either leave the house and do something or go mad from staring at the walls replaying the devastating scenes with her husband and former best friend, all the while wondering what she had done to deserve this.

'Hi Stella. I didn't know you were here.' Mercy slipped off her sunglasses and immediately raised a hand to shield her eyes from the glare of the sun. The afternoon heat and humidity had made watching the match particularly challenging and while the game was suspended for half-time, the players huddled under the shade of a nearby tree to gulp down water and suck on fresh orange wedges.

'I was standing over there.' Stella gestured to the other side of the pitch. 'I tried to attract your attention, but you were lost in thought, so I waited until the boys took a break.'

Jamie, Stella's son, and Hakeem had been close friends since starting primary school together a year earlier. Much like their sons, Mercy and Stella had hit it off from the start and had quickly become good friends. But her outings with Stella since Araba's return from London had dwindled to the occasional coffee and a friendly wave whenever they ran into each other at school. It hadn't taken long, Mercy now acknowledged wretchedly, for Stella to join the list of people she had stupidly allowed Araba to monopolise out of her life.

'Hey, are you okay?' Stella frowned. 'You don't look very well.' The furrows in her brow deepened as Mercy's eyes instantly filled with tears. Stella glanced around the group of people congregated around the pitch, grabbed Mercy's arm and pulled her away. Without a word, Stella led her to a cool spot under the shade of an acacia tree and carefully positioned herself to shield her friend from curious eyes while Mercy sobbed uncontrollably.

After a few minutes, Mercy gulped and forced herself to stop crying, fumbling with shaking fingers for the tissues she'd wisely stuffed into her handbag. Stella watched in silence while her friend dried her tears and attempted to regain her composure before asking tentatively, 'What's going on? I've never seen you like this. What's upset you – is it Lucas?'

Mercy swallowed hard, mortified at losing control in a public place. Thank *God* none of Hakeem's friends had seen her! 'I'm so sorry. I didn't mean to fall apart like that. I thought I could – could handle this, but—'

'Handle what?' Stella broke in, looking perplexed. 'Is it the pressure from all the campaigning for the elections?'

Mercy shook her head and forced a laugh which even to her own ears rang hollow. She thought of Lucas's threats – there was no other word for it – if she told anyone about their situation. But then she remembered Araba's unrepentant betrayal and threw caution to the winds.

* * *

'Well, you know what they say: there are none so blind as those who choose not to see,' Stella remarked before swallowing the last few drops of her milky coffee.

'What do you mean?' Mercy responded sharply. She was beginning to question the wisdom of sharing the events of the past week with Stella, but after unburdening herself for most of the past hour they'd spent in the coffee shop after dropping Jamie and Hakeem at Stella's, it was a bit late to worry about that. Besides Stella had always been a good friend – her best friend, in fact, until Araba had thrust herself back into the top spot and sidelined any rivals.

As if Stella could read minds, she said thoughtfully, 'Araba has been very good at keeping people away from you. At first I thought she was jealous of our friendship, but then I realised she probably doesn't rate me enough to feel jealous. I guess when your uncle will soon be President, little people like me don't even feature on your radar.'

'She's never really been what you'd call a woman's woman, and I suppose she's got into the habit of being protective of me,' Mercy explained, wondering why, even now, she still felt the need to defend Araba.

'It looked more like possessive than protective to me.' Stella shrugged. 'But, then again, she's not really my cup of tea. She gets very intense sometimes and makes me feel quite uncomfortable.'

Stella paused and then gave Mercy a wry smile. 'But she also seems to have a knack for getting exactly what she wants, doesn't she? Let's be honest, Mercy, when was the last time you came over to my house – and not just to drop off Hakeem, but to stay and chat? And I can't remember when we last went out for our Friday evening drinks.'

Mercy flushed and fiddled with her coffee mug. Stella was right, but Araba had always been the dominant partner in their friendship, and it had been easier to concede to her demands for Mercy's undivided attention than to argue with her. 'I'm sorry. I should have stood up to her and made time for our friendship. But looking back, it just feels like she was *always* around.'

Stella sighed. 'Mercy, I tried to tell you there was something not right about the way she behaves around Lucas, but you didn't want to hear it. She's been practically living in your house, even when you're not at home. It's like she's got no idea of boundaries – I've seen her at parties always hanging around you and Lucas. She's forever dragging him off into corners to talk about politics and never seems to give a damn about how it looks.'

'I've never had a sister,' Mercy said weakly. 'I just thought her coming and going as she likes was a sign of how close we were.'

Stella pushed her cup to the side with a groan. 'Oh my *God*! You really are far too sweet and trusting for your own good. If my sister behaved like that around my husband, I'd slap her!'

Mercy had been swallowing the dregs of her coffee, and she spluttered with laughter, almost choking in the process. Stella leaned forward and took Mercy's hands between hers. 'The woman's a bitch, pure and simple. You trusted her and she took advantage of that trust. But now you have to think about you – and what's best for you and Hakeem.'

At the mention of Hakeem, Mercy rapidly sobered up. 'Lucas says he'll divorce me if I cause him any trouble *and* take custody of Hakeem. He's obsessed with the Party and I honestly think he'll do whatever it takes to shut me up.'

Stella's eyes widened. 'What, you mean he'd actually *hurt* you?' She released Mercy's hands and leaned back in her chair, clearly shocked.

'I'm beginning to realise that man is capable of anything. I've been so cocooned in my perfect, sheltered world that I was clueless about what was happening around me.'

For a moment there was silence, and then Mercy added, 'I was offered a job last week, you know.'

Stella raised an eyebrow. 'You want to go out to work?'

'I've *always* wanted to work, but Lucas kicked up such a fuss whenever I mentioned it that I gave in. I used to think it was because he wanted to look after me, and now I realise that it was just his way of keeping me under his control. Now he's got Araba—' she broke off and swallowed painfully, 'I thought he wouldn't care if I went back to work, but yesterday when I told him Max Bamford has offered me a writing job, he said no. Just like that, no.

I can't work for Bamford Media because *he* doesn't trust Max. How ironic is that? Oh, and of course it would send the wrong message to the Party and to the public when we're so close to elections.'

Stella touched Mercy's arm sympathetically. 'So, what are you going to do?'

'Hakeem is my world, Stella, you know that. I can't risk losing him, and anyway Lucas is right about me not having a choice. Without a job, I've no money of my own, so where would I go? Besides, how can I fight Lucas and win, especially once the Party is in power – you know how things work here.'

* * *

Driving back home with an excited Hakeem in the back seat chattering non-stop, Mercy felt better for having told Stella the truth. She'd missed their forthright conversations and the uncomplicated relationship they had forged before Araba's return. But listening to Stella had also forced Mercy to acknowledge that she couldn't simply lay the blame for her slow drift away from her friends at Araba's feet. As the only one of her fellow university graduates without a job outside the home, Mercy had been feeling increasingly isolated even before Araba's return. Listening to her friends' complaints about irritating bosses, difficult subordinates and frustrating office politics had left her torn between feeling defensive about her situation and simply feeling left out. While no one voiced any criticism of her decision to stay at home, Mercy had keenly felt the fact that her identity was solely as Lucas's wife.

Araba's return had given her someone she could latch on to without feeling judged and, once again, she had used their friendship to fill the void created by her own insecurities. But facing the truth didn't change her situation or offer her a way out. Now, without Araba, Mercy realised more than ever just how lonely her life had become.

Chapter 4

It took Hakeem several minutes to say goodbye to Jamie, and Mercy watched her son hoist his rucksack, brand new only two weeks earlier when term had started and already streaked with mud, over one shoulder before finally walking away. Even at ten, it was obvious Hakeem was destined to grow as tall as the relatives on his father's side, and it wouldn't be long before she would have to look up when speaking to her boy.

With a final wave to Jamie, Hakeem loped over to where Mercy sat waiting in the back seat of the car. Along with the other areas of her life over which she had relinquished control, Mercy no longer drove her son to and from school. That particular duty was accorded to her driver, Ismail, who had been instructed to take the Minister's wife wherever she needed to go – and report her movements to the Minister at the end of each day.

It had been three years since the Party swept into power, winning the elections with an unprecedented landslide and dashing Mercy's secret hopes and silent prayers. Once the results had been verified, adhering to Lucas's instructions, she had pasted a sweet smile on to her face and attended the inauguration party and all the other festivities, dancing with her husband and looking every inch the perfect wife. She had even managed a gracious smile when greeting Araba in public, despite knowing that everyone present was aware the woman was Lucas's mistress. By focusing on a mental picture of her son, Mercy had kept her side of the bargain in public, saving her tears for her pillow during the long nights she slept alone.

Following Lucas's appointment as Senior Minister and Special Advisor to the President, Mercy's life had become a gilded cage. Along with her personal chauffeur, there was no shortage of luxuries available to her through Lucas's credit card, all of which left her feeling trapped, suffocated and increasingly worthless. Having unrestricted access to the latest fashions and the best restaurants in the city had proved no substitute for losing the marriage she had once treasured. It had become commonplace for Lucas to return home from work to eat dinner with them, and then spend some time with his son before heading out again. He rarely offered an explanation, and Mercy knew better than to ask. Besides, she knew exactly where he was going.

'Mum, you're not listening!' Hakeem's plaintive voice broke into her thoughts.

'I'm sorry, my love, what did you say?' She reached out to pat down a stray lock of his hair and he ducked his head out of her reach in outrage. She bit back a sigh; even her baby no longer welcomed the affection she enjoyed lavishing on him.

'What were you asking me, Hakeem?'

Satisfied she wasn't going to attempt another assault upon his person, he continued, 'What are you doing for your birthday? Why don't you have a party like Kojo's mum did? He said they had more than fifty people in their house. She had a *huge* chocolate cake with four layers – he brought some to class.'

'Do you want me to have a birthday party or do you just want cake?' Mercy laughed. 'I don't know, son. You know, Auntie Stella's also suggested I should have a party, but I'm not really sure I want—'

He broke in impatiently. 'Mum, you spend too much time at home just taking care of me and Daddy. It's your *birthday*! It's time you did something for yourself, for a change.'

Mercy cocked her head to one side and scrutinised his earnest expression. What did they say about wisdom coming from the mouths of babes? Suddenly, she felt the urge to tug at the threads tying her into a life of aimless luxury and to strike out for a change. What was the point of having a big house and a wealthy husband if she didn't spoil herself? From what she'd heard through the grapevine, Lucas was certainly sparing no expense when it came to Araba.

'You know what, son? Maybe you're right. Okay, let's do it! I'll call Auntie Stella tomorrow and tell her I'm taking her up on her promise to plan everything.'

'Oh, and, um, Mum… don't forget the cake!'

* * *

Almost every inch of the perfectly manicured lawn was covered in tables draped in white linen. Having packed the ground floor of the house, her guests had now spilled out onto the terrace steps and Mercy moved among them, smiling sweetly while urging them down into the garden to take their seats for the buffet dinner. Through the glass patio doors, she could see Stella inside jollying along the waiters who had been tasked with circulating between the tables with crates of drinks nestling in crushed ice. Stella had run her own events company for years and, true to her word, she had organised everything from caterers and equipment hire to the live band now playing on the far side of the terrace.

'Happy birthday!'

Mercy spun around at the sound of the deep familiar voice and beamed. '*Max*! I'm so glad you could come!'

He smiled and drew her into a warm hug, releasing her just as she felt herself burrowing into his muscular hold. 'How could I not? After all, how often do I get an invitation into the hallowed sanctum of the Senior Minister's house?'

She wrinkled her nose at him. 'Be nice, it's my birthday. What's that in your hand?'

He chuckled and handed over an extravagantly wrapped package. 'Just a small token of my affection, and to wish you a very happy birthday.'

She tugged at the ribbons and opened the box, gasping at the sleek silver chain bracelet with a diamante star-shaped charm nestling against the blue velvet that lined the box. 'Oh, Max,' she breathed. 'It's beautiful!' She slipped it over her wrist and looked up with a wide smile which faltered at the expression on his face. It was a curious blend of pain and longing, and she shivered at the naked desire she suddenly saw in his eyes. Then, as if she'd imagined it, he grinned and touched her lightly on the shoulder before following the other guests down into the garden.

She could still feel the warmth of Max's fingers on her skin as Lucas approached her with a frown. 'Did you actually invite that man here?'

She raised her chin defiantly. 'Why not? Max is an old friend – and besides, it's my party and I can invite anyone I choose.'

His face darkened, but whether it was the two glasses of wine she'd already put away, or the look in Max's eyes that reminded her that she was still a desirable woman, Mercy didn't care.

Whatever Lucas planned to say was interrupted by Stella's appearance. 'Oh, Mercy, there you are! You and the Minister should take your places – most of the guests are seated now.'

'Thanks, Stella.' Mercy smiled. She turned to Lucas and added sweetly, 'Minister, are you ready?' Without waiting for a reply, she extended her hand and he reluctantly took it and led the way down into the garden, nodding and smiling at the guests applauding them all the way to the top table.

* * *

Almost an hour later, Mercy tipped back the remains of her wine and gestured to the waiter for a refill.

'Don't you think you've had enough?' Lucas muttered as soon as the waiter moved away.

'It's my party and I'll drink if I want to,' Mercy retorted. 'Why so grumpy, my darling – are you missing your precious Araba? I'm surprised you didn't invite her to join us. After all, she's such a big part of our marriage.'

'Keep your voice down!'

'Oh *puh-leese*! Do you think there's a single person here who doesn't know about the two of you?' She swallowed a large mouthful of the chilled white wine and gave a mirthless laugh. 'The only mystery is why I still put up with it. And we both know the answer to that one, don't we, my *darling* husband?'

'You're drunk!' he said accusingly.

'Yep! It's by far the best way to get through this farce of a marriage,' she mocked, taking another defiant gulp.

With a snort of disgust, Lucas turned his back on her and was soon deep in conversation with the elderly Vice President, the special guest Lucas had insisted on inviting. *Typical Lucas!* had been Mercy's first thought when he'd made the announcement. It was common knowledge that her husband was tipped to take over as Vice President if the Party won a second term in two years and, as far as she was concerned, it was utterly graceless to make a show of the man he had every intention of displacing.

Bored rigid by the guests seated at her table, most of whom were Party dignitaries with whom she had only a nodding acquaintance, Mercy excused herself and returned to the house to check on Hakeem. Her son, disgusted at being sequestered in his bedroom during the party he had suggested, had only been pacified by the promise of a massive hunk of cake. As Mercy walked into the deserted hallway, she spotted Max heading purposefully for the front door.

'You're not leaving already, are you?' she exclaimed with disappointment.

He stopped in his tracks and turned around with a rueful smile. 'I was hoping to slip away without being noticed. I've got an early meeting tomorrow to prepare for.'

'But I was hoping for a dance with you later,' she pouted. She held his gaze and walked slowly towards him until her body was only inches away from his. Fortified by the wine, she could feel her inhibitions slipping away, and her eyes issued an unspoken challenge.

'Then maybe it's just as well I'm going. I'm not sure I could behave myself if I was holding you in my arms,' he remarked, the amusement in his voice so completely at odds with the intensity in his eyes that a surge of pure heat pulsed through her.

For a long moment they observed each other in silence. Then Mercy said softly, 'Why do you always tease, Max? If you really wanted to be with me, you had your chance when we were at university. You knew how I felt about you then, and for a while I thought you felt the same.' She shook her head in bafflement. 'I've never understood why you suddenly went from chasing me to treating me like your buddy.'

Max raised an eyebrow, his expression incredulous. '*You* had feelings for me back then?'

'Of course, I did!' *I still do*, she thought silently. 'I thought everyone knew I had the biggest crush on you. Why do you think Lucas dislikes you so much – apart from the obvious reason that every politician in Ghana considers you a devil.'

He didn't respond to her weak attempt to lighten the conversation, but instead ran a hand over his neatly cropped hair with a heavy sigh. 'Mercy, I promise you that I had no idea. I liked you – a lot. Truth be told, I was crazy about you, but Araba was adamant you weren't interested in me and that it would make things awkward between us if I asked you out. I didn't want to lose you, and if that meant keeping you in the friend zone, I was prepared to hold my peace. By the time I'd worked up the courage to try again, Lucas had swept you off your feet and there was really no point in speaking up and ruining a good friendship.'

Mercy groaned silently. *Araba, again!* Not content with stealing her husband, the woman had also prevented Max from pursuing a relationship which Mercy knew without a shadow of a doubt would have brought her infinitely more happiness than life with Lucas had done.

As if regretting having been so frank, Max flashed his customary grin and said in a resolute tone, 'Anyway, that's all in the past. Look at you now – the happily married wife of the man most likely to be our country's next Vice President.'

She cocked her head to one side and eyed him. 'Happily married?' she echoed sardonically. 'Don't insult me by pretending you don't know about my husband and Araba.'

For a moment Max looked pained, and then he shrugged. 'I don't understand why you're still with him, if you really want to know what I think, but it's none of my business.'

He made as if to walk away, and then stopped and said brusquely, 'Look, forget everything I just said about back in the day. Right now, there's a job open for you in my media team if you want it. Maybe when you're financially independent, you'll feel more able to – I don't know, make your own choices.' He inhaled sharply and then added dryly, 'I'd better go before I say too much.'

He opened the front door and she followed him outside. Her guests were still enjoying dinner in the garden, and the front entrance and driveway were deserted, the security personnel having been stationed at the end of the long drive to guard the fleet of luxury vehicles parked outside the gates. She stopped for a moment to breathe in the heady night air, perfumed by the beds of flowers and hibiscus bushes surrounding the house.

'Good night, Mercy, and happy birthday again.' Max leaned in to kiss her cheek and she turned her head just as his lips grazed her skin, capturing his lips with hers before he had a chance to pull away.

For a moment, she felt him resist, and then he slipped his arm around her and pulled her hard against him, kissing her with an intensity that set her head spinning. For several moments, they stood locked together, tasting each other hungrily, until Mercy pulled away with a gasp. Despite the wine she'd been drinking all evening, she knew it wasn't the alcohol that had spurred her action.

'I'm *so* sorry, Max! I shouldn't have done that. I—'

He placed a finger gently on her lips. 'Shush, it's okay. It was just as much my fault. I'd better go.'

Holding back the sob rising in her throat, Mercy watched him stride down the dark driveway until he was out of sight, forcing herself not to run after him. She stroked the silver bracelet on her wrist and for a few minutes allowed herself the luxury of imagining what a life with Max would have been like. She could have wept at the bitter irony of her situation; without Araba's interference, Mercy might have had a life with a husband who was both faithful and ethical, one who'd have encouraged her professionally and – and *loved* her.

* * *

'*Pho-toh-grapher!* Oo, Lyla, your friend sounds *very* posh! Stella, please ask the pho-toh-grapher to take our picture. I must remember to say it properly – unfortunately, those of us who only schooled in Ghana pronounce it *photographer.*' Mercy stressed the third syllable, ignoring Lyla's discomfited expression and pretending not to see the momentary flash of contempt on the face of the beautiful woman Lyla had brought and introduced as her childhood friend. *What was her name again? Ah, Theresa!*

Mercy knew she was behaving badly. Lyla, who lived with her husband a couple of streets away in Marula Heights, was one of the few friends who hadn't gravitated towards Lucas and Araba while still pretending to sympathise with Mercy. But after Max's abrupt departure and several more glasses of wine, she really didn't care. Something about Theresa's low-pitched, British-accented voice suggesting they take a picture together had instantly reminded Mercy of Araba and prompted her to lash out.

With a nervous laugh, Stella broke the awkward silence by quickly gesturing to the waiting cameraman. As soon as he'd taken the snap, Lyla offered a terse word of thanks and ushered Theresa out of the hall.

Watching the women head outside to return to their table, Mercy bit her lip, feeling utterly mortified at her bitchy and unprovoked dig at Theresa. Lyla had always been friendly towards her and she was the last person Mercy wanted to offend. A passing waiter attempted to refill her glass, but Mercy waved him away and walked out onto the terrace, suddenly desperate for fresh air. *Pull yourself together, Mercy. You need all the friends you can get.* Just because she was miserable didn't give her the right to treat other people badly, particularly when they were guests in her home.

The music from the band playing close by was too loud for comfort and Mercy stumbled down the stone steps and made her way towards a deserted area to the side of the house, weaving as the effects of the wine took hold. Turning the corner, she blinked at the sight of Lucas on his phone, his body partly concealed by a cluster of flowering shrubs. She had no doubt he was speaking to Araba and as the unfairness of her own situation hit her afresh, Mercy felt a surge of pure despair course through her.

Seeing Mercy approach, Lucas ended the call and slipped his phone into his shirt pocket. She winced at the look of irritation that descended on to his face, his default expression when he was forced to speak to her.

'Lucas why are you doing this to me?' she pleaded. 'If you want to be with her, go. Just go. Let's divorce and—'

'I've told you before, I don't want a divorce!' His tone was harsh and uncompromising. 'There are more important things to consider than your petty jealousy.'

'Maybe it's petty to you, but all this – it's *humiliating* to me!' she burst out. 'If you don't care about my feelings, think about Hakeem. How do you think he'll feel when he hears how you've treated me, his own mother?'

'For Christ's sake, Mercy, keep your voice down! There's no need for Hakeem to know anything unless, of course, you force me into divorcing you.'

51

Mercy blinked back the tears threatening to spill down her cheeks. There was no point crying in front of this unfeeling man who would rather hurt his only son by tearing him away from his mother than agree to a quiet separation. How could she have lived with him for so long and yet been so unaware that Lucas had neither heart nor conscience, she marvelled. Like all bullies, he only respected force – and people just like him who had no scruples or principles. *It's my own fault. I let him do this to me*. The thought flitted through her mind, but this time she faced it head on. This situation couldn't continue. Even if by some miracle Lucas was to agree to a divorce, where could she go and what would she do? Most importantly, after seeing the contents of that awful folder and knowing what she did about her husband, if anything happened to him, how would she take care of her son?

Emboldened by the copious amount of wine she'd consumed and disgusted at who she had let herself become, Mercy drew herself up to her full height and stared directly into her husband's eyes, making no attempt to disguise her loathing for him.

'If you won't agree to a divorce without us having to put Hakeem through the ordeal of a custody battle, then fine. But I'm tired of playing by your rules. If you insist on living your life the way you choose, then so shall I.'

He glared at her. 'What are you talking about? You'd better remember your position as my wife. The Party—'

'*Screw* the Party! I want my life back, Lucas, and if you try to stop me, we'll just have to see who wins.'

Relishing the stunned expression on her husband's

face, Mercy turned and walked back towards the terrace and into the house, her heart jumping giddily at the unfamiliar sensation of rebellion. She held onto the banisters for support as she hurried up the wide circular staircase and into her bedroom. Snatching her mobile from the drawer of her dressing table, she sat on the bed and punched the handset with trembling fingers.

As soon as Mercy heard the call connect, her words burst out unchecked. 'It's me. The answer's yes! Yes, Max, I want the job.'

Chapter 5

Mercy looked up from her computer and glanced around the empty office. It was well past the end of the working day and with no witnesses around to wonder if she'd lost her mind, she let out a loud squeal of pure joy. Her smile widened as she took in the large open-plan room with its rows of work stations surrounded by double-glazed glass-partitioned cubicles which served as offices for Max and his senior team. The office walls were covered in notices, press releases and shift rotas, as well as several whiteboards on which upcoming productions and project deadlines had been scribbled in black, blue and red markers.

It was almost six months since Mercy had started work at Bamford Media, and she had never been happier. Coming to work each day had restored the sense of purpose which had seeped away slowly over the years, finally disappearing on the day she discovered Araba and Lucas's affair.

Despite her euphoria at the idea of earning her own living, returning to work after a decade as a full-time housewife had been terrifying. Her first week as a member of Max's close-knit professional team had merged into a blur as she tried to get to grips with technology she had never even heard of. Grappling with unfamiliar computer systems at the same time as trying to understand electronic message boards and master complex research databases, Mercy had felt like an alien who'd landed on a planet where everyone looked like her but spoke a completely different language. But, whatever she had lacked in technological skills, she'd more than made up for in her enthusiasm to learn and her willingness to work as hard and as late as possible without neglecting Hakeem. Only too aware that the team knew her as the boss's friend (not to mention the wife of a high-profile government minister), she had been determined to prove herself in her own right and earn the respect of her colleagues. Guided by Sylvia, Max's seasoned head of editorial content, Mercy's writing skills which had grown rusty from a lack of use, had quickly improved, and before long she was entrusted with producing independent copy for several of the programmes in production. Within a few weeks, she'd found herself collaborating with Bamford Media's most experienced researchers and producers to craft high-quality content and scripts for new documentaries and other TV programming, including Max's flagship political show. The sheer number of projects swamped her days and evenings, and she regularly brought work home to meet the challenging deadlines, putting in extra time after Hakeem had gone to bed.

Lucas's absences no longer bothered her – in fact, Mercy couldn't wait for dinner to be over so he could leave. But while her professional life had taken a welcome turn, her personal life was utterly stagnant. After several abortive attempts to deter her from working for Max, Lucas had given up trying and their lives had fallen into a pattern of little to no communication, unless Hakeem was present. Her son was growing fast, and Mercy knew he would soon question the nature of his parents' relationship. Until then, she was determined to maintain appearances while she focused on building a career that would allow her to protect and take care of her child. The images she had saved on to her phone that fateful day three years earlier were a constant reminder that she could take nothing for granted.

In the years since the election, however, Lucas's career had flourished, and his profile had been further raised by introducing new social programmes to tackle poverty and unemployment. The President, ignoring the Opposition's accusations of nepotism, had appointed Araba as a Special Trade Envoy to lead on international trade negotiations, and she was frequently televised travelling on trade missions and attending government functions. Lucas was rarely far from her side and their relationship was an open secret within official circles. Much to Mercy's disgust, it had become apparent that Lucas's popularity had trumped the Party's much-vaunted family values platform.

Even Mercy's mother-in-law, who she had hoped would at least see her side of things, and maybe even talk some sense into her son, had metaphorically shrugged off Lucas's behaviour, dismissing Mercy's fears that Hakeem would discover his father's affair through a school mate or social media gossip.

'My dear, you have to accept men are weak and that any woman can come along and turn their heads. You can't control your husband, so it's up to you as the wife to protect your home and your family.'

'But how can I do that when Lucas blatantly disrespects me and flaunts his mistress shamelessly,' had been Mercy's frustrated response to the older woman's unfair reasoning.

But if Lucas remained a problem, so too did Max, although for entirely different reasons. Since she'd joined Bamford Media, Max's attitude towards Mercy had been entirely professional and with no sign of his customary teasing or flirtatiousness, even on those occasions when they found themselves working late and alone in the office. It was as if the kiss they had shared on the night of her birthday party had never happened, and if occasionally Mercy imagined a look in his eyes that suggested otherwise it was always so fleeting that she could never be sure. But while Max was doing a sterling job of keeping up his guard, Mercy struggled to follow suit. His revelations on that fateful night had ripped away the protective shield she had placed over her feelings for him, and she replayed the kiss constantly in her mind. She knew instinctively that Max still felt something for her, but while she sometimes wished he would admit it, she also feared the consequences of stirring up a situation which could only complicate her life and potentially hurt Hakeem.

The shrill tone of her mobile jolted Mercy out of her thoughts and she reached for the phone to answer Hakeem's call, a heartfelt plea for the imported sweets his father occasionally brought home. She glanced at her watch, and sighed. Swanson's was the only shop Mercy knew that stocked the sweets and she generally avoided using the luxury supermarket, associating it indelibly in her mind with the day her life, as she'd known it, had ended.

But, only too aware she would get no peace from her son if she went home without them, Mercy reluctantly switched off her computer and picked up her bag before heading out of the building to her car. With no further need of his services unless she was on official duty, Ismail had long since been reassigned, and Mercy drove herself out of the office complex to join the heavy traffic heading towards Osu. It was almost closing time when she finally arrived at Swanson's, and she had no trouble finding parking. Hurrying into the shop, she plucked two small bags of sweets off the shelf, grimacing at the exorbitant prices on the stickers. Despite his public pronouncements about the need to support local industries, it was typical of Lucas to do exactly the opposite by over-indulging his son with expensive imported treats.

Her eyes continued to linger over the other goodies on the shelf as she turned around, and she cannoned straight into another shopper. Mercy's words of apology froze on her lips as she came face to face with Araba, who gave an involuntary gasp.

Other than politely murmured greetings when their paths occasionally crossed at official functions, it had been three years since the two women had spoken, and each silently scrutinised the other. Mercy's eyes roved critically over her former friend, noting the shadows under Araba's almond-shaped eyes and new tiny lines radiating from the sides. The long glossy braids couldn't disguise a few threads of silver visible at her temples, and her cheeks looked hollow, making her high cheekbones appear even more pronounced. *She looks in need of a good meal and some sleep*, Mercy mused. She maintained her composure as Araba's gaze raked over her in turn, scanning Mercy's fitted cobalt-blue linen dress with raised eyebrows. Working long hours and dealing with the emotional shipwreck of her marriage had transformed Mercy's once plump curves into a petite, slender physique. While she would never be skinny, Mercy no longer hated the sight of her body in the mirror or felt inadequate when compared to women like the one in front of her.

Concluding her inspection, Araba gave a tiny nod of acknowledgement and remarked dryly, 'Well, this is a surprise.'

Mercy shrugged. 'It's a small town; it was bound to happen sometime, I suppose.'

'You're looking well.'

'Don't sound so surprised, Araba. Do you expect me to be drowning in a pool of my own tears every day because of what you and Lucas get up to?'

Araba's eyes flashed with malice. 'Who knows? If you're anything like your mother, anything's possible.'

Mercy bit her tongue, refusing to give Araba the satisfaction of rising to the bait. 'I see you're still as charming as ever,' she said mildly. 'Well, I'd like to say it's been a pleasure, but I try to speak the truth. One liar in my home is already more than enough.'

With that, Mercy stepped aside but before she could go any further, Araba quickly moved to block her path. 'Wait!'

Mercy watched a series of emotions flit across Araba's face, curious about where this was leading. Finally, a look that blended defiance and pleading settled on the other woman's face and she blurted out, 'I need to talk to you.'

Mercy arched an eyebrow. 'Oh? What about?'

'Lucas, of course. Look, Mercy, we both know this situation has gone on for long enough. It's obvious your marriage is over, and it's time that Lucas and I were together properly. I know you don't want a divorce, but—'

'*I* don't want a divorce?' For a moment Mercy stared in disbelief, and then she dissolved into laughter, ignoring the darkening expression on the other woman's face. 'Oh my God, is *that* what he's told you? Oh dear, you really should take Lucas's statements with a big pinch of salt and remember that once a liar, always a liar.'

'What are you talking about?' Araba snapped.

'I've been literally begging Lucas for a divorce since I found out he was cheating on me with you,' Mercy said, trying to stop the giggles still threatening to escape. 'He's refused point blank.'

Araba's lips tightened. 'I don't believe you. And even if that were true, he probably doesn't want to damage his chances at the next elections.'

The urge to laugh instantly disappeared, and Mercy eyed her soberly. 'Really? Right now, your precious Party and half the country think Lucas practically walks on water, so I don't think a quiet, civilised divorce would damage his standing in the slightest.'

'Then—?'

'Your guess is as good as mine, Araba. If you can persuade him to agree to a divorce that gives me full custody of Hakeem, then trust me, I will not stand in the way.'

Araba curled her lip. 'Why – because of Max Bamford? I've heard you work for him now. When did that little love affair get rekindled?'

'You know perfectly well it was never an affair – thanks to you.'

'Oh, so he told you, did he? Well, he couldn't have been that keen if he gave up on you so easily,' Araba sneered.

Mercy bit her lip and forced her voice to remain even. 'You can think what you like, but I work for Max and that's all. Get Lucas to agree to a divorce where I get custody of my son, and you can have the man for all I care.'

Mercy made to walk away, and once again Araba stopped her. 'Hakeem is Lucas's son too, you know. Maybe he'll want him to live with us after *we* get married...' she tailed off at the look of undisguised fury Mercy turned on her.

'You managed to take my husband, Araba, but I'll kill you before I allow you to take my son!'

Incensed at the sheer nerve of the woman, Mercy raised her hand and pushed Araba out of the way before stalking to the cash register, shaking with fury. Driving home, she turned on the radio to calm her agitation and listened in dismay as the newscaster reported on the latest national polls placing the Party well ahead of the Opposition. The polls also tipped Lucas as the runaway favourite for Vice President, and a shoo-in for President when the country next went to the polls. *Over my dead body!* Mercy thought angrily. Never far from her mind were the pictures she had taken that day in Lucas's study, and the shocking contents of the folder were incontrovertible evidence of who Lucas really was;

a man who was totally unfit to lead her beloved country.

Araba's needling was the last straw, Mercy thought grimly. The only thing both women agreed on was that this situation had gone on long enough and it was time to go ahead with the plan she'd been brewing for months. Recognising that she was about to take a huge gamble which could backfire and hurt both her and Hakeem, Mercy also knew she had no choice. If Lucas wasn't stopped now, it would soon be too late. But in order to do what she knew had to be done, Mercy needed help from someone she could trust, someone who knew how the system worked. It didn't take much thinking to reach the obvious conclusion that the only person who fitted the bill was Max.

* * *

'What the—? Mercy, where the *hell* did you get these?'

Max couldn't have looked more shocked if Mercy had shown him a picture of herself dancing naked on a table in a crowded nightclub.

She grimaced as she watched him scroll through the hastily snapped documents on her phone. 'I found them all in a folder in Lucas's desk. He has no idea I've seen them – I'm sure about that because I'd probably be dead in a ditch if he thought I had the slightest idea.'

Max shook his head, visibly shaken by the images. 'Don't even joke about something like that. There are some powerful people here who wouldn't think twice about arranging exactly that.'

She gave a weak smile which was met with a frown. 'I mean it, Mercy. You can't tell anyone about these. Forward them all to me and delete everything. If Lucas gets hold of your phone and finds them, there's no telling what he'll do. Especially now you're working with me.'

'*For* you, boss,' she retorted. 'It's very kind of you to pretend I'm your equal but I'm a lowly staff writer and you're the head honcho, which is fine with me.'

'Okay, well since I'm the boss, let's be clear that neither you nor I are leaving this room until I know those images are off your phone, so send them to me now.'

Mercy sighed and took back the handset, rapidly forwarding all the documents she had photographed to Max's number. He checked his mobile and then looked on while she systematically deleted each one from her phone memory, exhaling audibly when she announced the last one gone.

'Thank God for that. Okay, so now tell me, what do you want me to do with them?'

Mercy sat in silence for a moment. She had no doubts about Lucas's unfitness for public office, given what she knew about him. But how would stopping Lucas affect those around him? She thought back to the conversation she'd had with Lucas's mother and replayed the acrimonious scene with Araba in Swanson's. Her mother-in-law had evidently made her peace with Lucas's behaviour and considered it Mercy's duty not to rock the boat. Araba, on the other hand, appeared desperate to resolve the murky status of her relationship with Lucas and clearly wouldn't hesitate to support him if he tried to take Hakeem. Where once she might have stopped to take account of their feelings, the bruising encounter with Araba had aroused the mother tiger in Mercy and banished any qualms about what she had to do. Neither of the two women had given a moment's consideration to either Mercy's feelings or Hakeem's best interests, and she was damned if she was prepared to consider theirs.

'Mercy, what do you want me to do with these pictures?' Max repeated.

This time Mercy replied without hesitation, her voice as unyielding as steel. 'I want you to use them to bring him down.'

Chapter 6

Mercy shrugged, careful not to sound too eager – the last thing she wanted was to arouse Lucas's suspicions – and answered truthfully. 'Because Max's talk show is the biggest platform for any politician in the country. The polls have you in the lead for VP and doing the show would give you a chance to sell your message to the country.'

'Why the hell would Bamford want to help me?' Lucas scoffed. 'From what I hear, he's still bitter that *I* got you and he didn't. Don't give me that look – I'm not an idiot. I've seen the way he looks at you, and I'd be a fool to give him the chance to trip me up on national television.'

Mercy sighed inwardly. This was proving harder than she'd expected. She knew her husband was no fan of Max Bamford, but she'd hoped appealing to Lucas's vanity would have overridden his dislike of the other man. While Lucas's insinuation that Max still cared for her was secretly thrilling to hear, she forced herself to focus on the task of getting her husband to agree to the interview. Her entire plan hinged on it.

'It wasn't Max's suggestion that you do the show,' Mercy pointed out. 'It was mine.' *Which was also true.* 'I just thought you'd welcome the opportunity to highlight the Party's successes and give viewers more insight into you as their next potential leader. We both know you're an excellent speaker and the public certainly seem to love you.'

Lucas appeared even more sceptical. 'And why are *you* suddenly so interested in enhancing my profile or promoting the government's achievements? You've made it perfectly clear how much you detest the Party.'

Mercy hesitated. There was no point protesting an affinity to the Party that they both knew wasn't true. If she was to persuade Lucas, she'd have to appeal to his way of thinking and his values – or rather, his lack of them. Her husband only respected money and power and, as far as he was concerned, no one did anything except for material gain.

'True, I'm no fan of the Party, but *I'm* not stupid, either. Working for Max isn't exactly earning me a fortune, and if you make Vice President, Hakeem and I will have access to the income and the prestige your position brings. Once you're in power, my son and I will be set for life.'

Lucas stared at her thoughtfully, and encouraged by his silence, she added, 'Look, I'll be working with the producers on the show and I'll also be right there during the live programme. If it makes you feel any better, I'll get you a copy of the questions Max will be asking before you go on.'

She held her breath while he thought through her suggestion. *Careful, Mercy. Don't overplay your hand.*

'Okay, I'll do it,' Lucas pronounced, and Mercy slowly released the air straining to escape her lungs. She had taken the first – and the most difficult – step. The rest would be up to Max.

* * *

As the clock ticked down to the start of the show, the atmosphere in the television studio was even more tense than usual, and Mercy stepped aside as the assistant producer edged past her hurriedly to confer with her boss. Max's production team was well accustomed to celebrities, with numerous high-profile guests ranging from prominent personalities to senior politicians having taken their seat in the black chair over the years. But the buzz around the Senior Minister's appearance was different to any that had come before.

Despite Lucas's extensive campaign appearances around the country, there was still an element of mystery surrounding the popular young politician who had appeared seemingly out of nowhere, swiftly building a sizeable business empire and then rapidly rising to the highest echelons of the ruling party. Rarely giving interviews – and then only to carefully selected media outlets – Lucas preferred to use his mass campaign rallies and social media platforms to promote his messages and the Party's policies. He studiously ignored questions about his private life and made only vague references to his business background, a position which generally went unchallenged by journalists who considered themselves lucky to interview him in the first place. Consequently, the news that Lucas Peterson was to appear on *The Bamford Report*, the most popular and trusted current affairs programme on air, had caused a stir not only across the news media, but throughout the country.

Mercy perched on a stool in the production room where she could see the set and listen to the live interview, ignoring the occasional curious glance coming her way from the production team, doubtless wondering about her role in securing the elusive minister's appearance on Max's platform. This would unquestionably be the highest-rated show of the series, and more staff than was usual had crowded into the stuffy control room.

With everyone's attention on checking sound, lighting and camera angles, no one had time to talk to her, which was just as well. As the start time neared and her apprehension rose, Mercy was struggling to keep her breathing under control, and her palms felt damp and clammy. Terrified that the stress would provoke an asthma attack, she strove to calm her racing thoughts. *Come on, Mercy, breathe... slowly does it.*

'Hey, are you okay?'

Mercy opened her eyes to see Max standing in front of her, his brows drawn into a worried frown. She took a deep breath and exhaled slowly and then nodded. They had come this far, and she wasn't going to mess things up now.

Max glanced around at the organised chaos in the room and satisfied no one could hear, said in an undertone, 'If you're having second thoughts, it's not too late. We don't have to do this.'

Mercy glared at him and whispered fiercely, 'I'm *not* having second thoughts. I want you to do exactly as we planned. I mean it, Max!'

He hesitated, but then the producer pulled him aside with a muttered apology to Mercy, and there was no further opportunity to speak. Shortly afterwards Max left the room and Mercy watched him enter the studio and take his seat behind the desk. A double spotlight shone on to an imposing black leather armchair which had been placed on a red rug directly across from Max's desk, and

Mercy watched with her heart in her throat as Lucas strode into view and settled himself in the chair.

The production room fell silent as the producer slipped on his headphones and cued the music and opening titles, and Mercy leaned forward to stare intently at the two men on stage. The camera panned to Max as he smoothly welcomed viewers and introduced Lucas, his words piping clearly through the speakers mounted high on the wall into the room.

When the shot shifted to her husband, Mercy could tell instantly that he felt uneasy; Lucas was clutching the arms of the chair and his eyes blinked far more rapidly than usual. As if keen to put his guest at ease, Max opened with a series of straightforward questions delivered in a light-hearted and friendly manner, along with some humorous asides that soon had Lucas releasing his grip on the chair and visibly relaxing. Mercy watched him flash the smile that invariably charmed those who didn't know the real man while Max cleverly drew him out with questions that were probing but never too aggressive.

For the next forty minutes Mercy remained on her stool, transfixed, as the two men discussed Lucas's role in the Party and his vision for the country, with the occasional pause for commercials. Max continued to challenge Lucas enough to keep the man on his toes while still maintaining a good rapport with his guest and allowing him to make his points without undue interruption.

Mercy, on the other hand, was rapidly growing light-headed with anticipation. As Lucas's responses grew increasingly confident and occasionally, in her view, verging on the arrogant, Mercy's pulse raced even faster.

She'd seen Max in action enough times to know when he was building up to deliver a devastating blow. As if her thoughts had somehow been transmitted to him, Max leaned across the desk as his tone suddenly sharpened.

'Minister, it's probably fair to say that while people know of your successes since joining the Party, few of us know very much about your earlier life.

The camera panned to Lucas, and Mercy watched him straighten in his seat and a faintly wary expression descend on his smoothly attractive features. When Max didn't immediately follow up with a question, Lucas shrugged. 'I wouldn't say that. I mean, everyone knows I was a businessman before I became a politician.'

'That's true, Minister. However, you made a substantial fortune at a relatively young age and, it seems, almost overnight. What's your secret?'

Lucas shifted in his seat, his unease now clearly visible. 'There is no secret, I'm afraid,' he replied, with a chuckle that sounded strained. 'Just a lot of hard work setting up a thriving farm and then building a successful food processing company. Along the way, I've invested in several up-and-coming agribusiness ventures – in fact, I pride myself on giving back to others by investing seed capital into promising enterprises and mentoring new business owners.'

Smiling benignly, Max persisted. 'That's very laudable, Minister. However, coming back to how you got your own start, it's remarkable that you were lucky enough to obtain capital at a time when banks were notoriously failing to lend. Did you manage to secure bank loans, or perhaps it was through investment from private individuals?

Lucas was blinking fast and despite the powder the make-up artist had applied during the last commercial break, the sheen of perspiration was visible on his forehead. He spoke quickly, almost stammering in his haste to get the words out. 'Look, er, Max, I think people are far more interested in the Party and our plans for this country than my early business success.'

Max's genial smile disappeared. 'Minister, don't you think people should know about the character of the man who, by all accounts, will be Vice President – and possibly even President – one day? Surely how you first made your money is relevant to understanding the kind of man you are?'

Mercy watched with satisfaction as Lucas continued to bluster while Max's features remained coolly impassive. *Now, Max, now!*

The camera zoomed on to Max as he reached to the side of his desk and picked up a plain folder, and Mercy held her breath. He opened the folder and stared at the top sheet for a long moment without saying a word. The lens quickly spun to Lucas who had crossed his arms protectively across his chest and was visibly sweating through the pristine white of his linen shirt. Mercy was reminded of a picture she had once seen of a deer staring into a car's headlights and she felt a fleeting pang of sympathy. Then it disappeared as she remembered her mission, and she returned her attention to Max, who was silently flicking through the papers in the folder.

'What the hell's going on?' the producer muttered, sounding utterly bewildered. He wasn't the only one.

What are you waiting for? Come on, Max! Mercy

willed him on, her nails digging into the palms of her hands as the silence on the set stretched out. Up in the production room, the atmosphere was so tense that she was convinced everyone could hear the pounding of her accelerated heartbeat.

Suddenly Max dropped the folder back onto the desk and turned his attention back to Lucas with an amiable smile. 'So Minister, perhaps you can share with the country some of your personal interests and hobbies. What does a busy man like yourself do to relax?'

Mercy stared at the men in utter dismay, unable to believe her ears. What the *hell* had just happened? Why had Max, of *all* people, bottled it? She'd put her faith in him and now it was over! Thanks to him, her one chance to rid the country of the threat from a Lucas Peterson presidency and protect her son from his father's reckless behaviour had just gone up in flames.

* * *

'I *trusted* you, Max! You promised me you'd finish him, and I trusted you! I needed you to help me keep Hakeem, and you *failed* me.'

The show had ended an hour earlier, and the studio was deserted, except for Mercy and Max – who had been uncharacteristically quiet during the post-programme debrief which had just concluded. Accepting the team's enthusiastic congratulations with a gracious nod, he had kept his contribution to the meeting brief and avoided Mercy's accusatory stare. Lucas had been chauffeured away in his official car within minutes of the credits rolling, and Mercy, whose fury had been steadily building during the team meeting, had scarcely waited for the door to close behind the last member of staff before letting loose.

Seemingly undaunted by the angry tirade being hurled at him, Max shook his head. 'I didn't fail you.' He raised a hand to stop her protest. 'Mercy, wait, please think about it for a moment. If I'd gone ahead with what you wanted and disgraced Lucas in front of the entire country, he would have lost his job, yes, but it would be you and Hakeem who would have suffered most. *You're* the one he's married to, not Araba, and it's your name that would have been dragged through the mud. Have you considered that people might think you were involved in his actions?'

Mercy gasped. 'But – but I'd never—'

'Yes, *I* know that,' Max cut in impatiently. 'But that's because I know the kind of person you are, and I also know you had zero knowledge of what he was up to and would never have gone along with it if you had. But just think about it – you've been married to him for over ten years and enjoyed all the benefits of his wealth. Can't you see how easily people could accuse you of being complicit? I know you're desperate to protect Hakeem, but this wasn't the way. If I'd exposed him this evening, that video would have been up on social media within minutes. Can you imagine what it would have been like for your son going in to school tomorrow?'

She stared at him dumbly, her eyes filling with frustrated tears at the sheer unfairness of it all. If Max was right – and she still didn't believe he was – it meant Lucas would get away with everything. For a moment Max stood stony-faced and then with a muffled expletive,

73

he stepped forward and wrapped his arms around her.

'Don't cry. *Please* don't cry,' he pleaded softly. 'We'll think of something else. I promise. There will be a better way to see justice done.'

She rested her forehead against his chest and quietly let the tears slide down her cheeks while he slowly rubbed her back as if she were a child in distress. Mercy wanted nothing more than to stay within the comforting warmth of Max's embrace, but this was not the time. She pulled back to wipe her palm fiercely against her cheeks, and then backed away from his embrace to perch on the edge of a desk.

For a moment Max watched her in silence, and then he shook his head. 'I was this close,' – he pinched his thumb and forefinger together – 'to exposing him. I had all the printouts from the photos in that dossier.' He gestured towards the blue folder peeking out of his briefcase. 'Believe me, I would have loved nothing more than to lay every single sheet of paper out on the desk for the camera to film. You know how I feel about corruption.' He gave a mirthless laugh and continued, 'not to mention that this would probably have been the biggest scoop of my career. But I didn't do it. Mercy, all I could think about was what exposing Lucas in that way would do to you and your son, and I simply couldn't do it. I know you're upset with me now, but I care far too much about you to be responsible for causing you any hurt.'

She studied the pink varnish on the toenails peeking out from her high-heeled sandals while she processed his words, and then looked up at him quizzically. 'So you care about me?'

Max released an irritated sigh. 'Of course I do. Don't pretend you don't know.'

'Well, I definitely thought you did that evening at my birthday party, but since then...' she tailed off, trying not to giggle at the look of discomfort that had settled onto his face. For once, the cool, unflappable Max Bamford looked undeniably flustered. Despite everything that had happened that evening, and the still unresolved problem of Lucas, Mercy suddenly experienced an unexpected rush of pure joy, and she could scarcely keep from smiling as she watched Max earnestly attempting to explain himself.

'Look, when I offered you the job I assured you I wouldn't take advantage of the situation, and I meant it,' he insisted. 'But that – that doesn't mean, you know, that I don't, well... *dammit*, Mercy, you know what I mean!'

It was most definitely time to put him out of his misery, she decided. Grinning openly, she jumped off the desk and went to him, reaching her arms up and around his neck to draw his head down until their faces were almost touching.

'Well, then maybe *I* can take advantage of you,' she teased softly. She could feel the warmth of his breath on her cheek and she slowly pulled him in further, brushing his lips with feather-light kisses. He groaned and pulled her tightly against him and for several minutes, only the sound of their fevered breathing could be heard.

The sound of a door slamming in the corridor broke the spell, and they jumped apart. Mercy smoothed down her dress and tried to regain her composure, while Max raked his fingers through his hair and took a deep breath. 'I do care, Mercy. Very much. I always have and,' he added ruefully, 'I suspect I always will. But you're still married to that man, and neither of us can afford to forget that.'

Mercy nodded. 'You're right.' She picked up her handbag and before he could stop her, she snatched the folder sticking out of his briefcase. He opened his mouth, but she forestalled any protest by gently placing a finger on his lips.

'Just because I kissed you doesn't mean I'm not still angry with you for blowing up my plan, Max. But you're absolutely right about one thing. I'm the one who's still married to Lucas and who still has a son to protect, and it's down to me to sort out my own mess.'

Chapter 7

Mercy's initial anger at Max for abandoning her plan had been tempered by their kiss, and it subsided even further as she reflected on his comments while driving back to Marula Heights. For the first time, she began to see Max's point about the flaws in the plan she'd devised which, in her anger at Lucas, had sounded both plausible and justified. Now, she could see that it had been short-sighted and foolhardy, not to mention dangerous. Bringing down Lucas in the way she had begged Max to do wouldn't only have damaged the Party; it would also have exposed his victims and damaged people's faith in the institutions of their hard-fought-for democracy. While her actions would have wrecked Lucas's leadership hopes, the price of humiliating her husband on the national stage would also have exposed her to charges of collusion, not to mention the painful task of explaining to her son why she had deliberately destroyed his father.

It was also sobering to realise that while she had never endorsed Lucas's actions, she had – albeit unwittingly – benefited from the fortune he had lavishly spent on himself and his family. Her car, designer clothes and foreign holidays, even the flat in Switzerland he'd bought for them shortly after Hakeem was born, had all been funded from the proceeds of his businesses, as had the pretty, detached bungalow in a quiet gated housing community he had bought for his mother, and the monthly allowance he paid her.

Mercy waited for the security guard to open the gates and then drove up the driveway to park under the carport. There was no sign of Lucas's Mercedes, which he still maintained for his private use, and when she walked through the door, the silence hung heavy inside the empty house. The hallway was brightly lit with the extravagant designer spotlights her husband had insisted on installing a few months earlier, overriding her protests that they were both overpriced and an unnecessary load on their already high energy bills, while also rejecting Hakeem's complaints that they would increase his global footprint. Despite his public 'man of the people' posturing, Lucas loved his luxurious lifestyle and saw no contradiction between his campaign rhetoric about bridging the yawning gap in the country between the rich and poor, and the way he chose to live.

The light clicks of her heels against the floor tiles echoed in the silent hallway and she slipped off her shoes and tossed them aside. With Hakeem safely out of the way at Stella's house enjoying a sleepover with Jamie, Mercy had no qualms about what she intended to do. Lucas was no doubt over at Araba's house, but Mercy was past caring about their relationship. She wasn't prepared to wait any longer to resolve the tangled mess of their lives, and the only thing that concerned her now was that he returned home immediately. Taking out her phone, she dialled Lucas's number and put it on loudspeaker while she paced the hallway waiting for the call to connect. Even though Max was right and publicly disgracing Lucas wasn't the answer, for both Hakeem's sake and her own, not to mention the country's, she would rather die than allow her husband the prize for which he had risked everything and everyone.

'Yeah, Mercy, what is it?'

'Wow, Lucas. Not even a thank you to me for getting you the biggest interview of your political career?' Even as she uttered the words, she was struck by the realisation that she would never have dared to speak so boldly to Lucas in the past.

Perhaps he thought so too, given the long moment of silence that ensued. Then she heard him sigh, and he replied curtly. 'Fine. *Thank you*. Why are you calling me – is there something wrong with Hakeem?'

'Is our son the only reason why I should be speaking to you? You know what, don't even bother to answer that – nothing you think or do should surprise me any more. Hakeem is fine, and he's staying over at Stella's house tonight. *You're* the reason I'm calling. I need you to come home right now.'

There was no doubting the annoyance in his voice. 'You're in no position to give me orders, Mercy. I'll see you in the morning.'

'No, you won't! You'll see me now, or you can read about what I want to discuss with you in tomorrow's newspapers instead.'

There was a long moment of silence, and then Lucas said viciously, 'I *knew* Bamford was up to something! What the hell have you done?'

Breathing in deeply to calm her sudden nerves, Mercy replied coolly, 'Nothing – yet. But if you don't come back now, I promise you that will change.'

She could hear a female voice in the background, and Mercy felt a frisson of shock. The voice was far too high-pitched to be Araba's and besides, now she thought about it, she remembered a news report that morning about Araba leading a delegation currently involved in trade talks in London. Mercy shook her head in disgust. Clearly Lucas wasn't content with only one mistress, and for a second she felt a flicker of sympathy for her former best friend.

'I'm on my way,' he snarled down the phone. 'And you'd better not have done anything stupid, or you'll regret it. I mean it, Mercy!'

* * *

Mercy wandered into the living room and placed her half-empty wine glass onto a side table while she settled herself into the corner of the plump leather sofa. It had been twenty minutes since her call to Lucas and she expected his arrival at any moment. Fortified by the glass and a half of chilled white wine she had retrieved from the fridge while waiting for her husband, her nerves had vanished, and she felt more than ready to do what was needed. She glanced at the blue folder she had placed on the side table earlier and patted it lightly to reassure herself.

A few minutes later, she heard the powerful engine of Lucas's car sweeping up their gravelled driveway and she took a deep breath and a sip of wine. She glanced at the framed copy of a much younger smiling Hakeem with his football trophy and thought back to the woman she had been at the time the photograph was taken. Sweet Mercy, a woman who trusted her handsome, successful husband and worshipped her savvy, confident best friend. She thought about the months of pure hell she had endured after discovering their affair, and the subsequent years spent in a fog of wounded loneliness, forced to play the loyal Party wife while mourning the betrayal of her husband and the woman she had loved. And then she remembered Max, and the lifeline he had thrown her of a job which had not only allowed her to generate her own income for the first time in a decade, but had restored her confidence and her sense of self-worth as a person in her own right – and as a desirable woman.

It had been the support of good friends like Stella and Max, a man who had willingly put Mercy's reputation and security ahead of his own ambitions, that had encouraged her to slowly build a new and more independent life. And now, only one thing remained if she was to truly liberate herself. Hakeem's crooked grin in the close-up photo reminded her of what was at stake as she heard the front door open and close, and her husband's rapid footsteps approaching. *You can do this, Mercy. You've got this.*

True to form, Lucas wasted no time on niceties. Striding into the room, he marched over to the sofa and fixed her with a ferocious glare.

Mercy stared back impassively, refusing to drop her gaze and lose the match before it had even started. 'You look like you got dressed in a hurry. Did my call catch you in the middle of something?' she remarked coolly.

His eyes flashed with anger. 'I thought you'd finally got it into your head that what I do is none of your business.

Spit it out, Mercy. What do you think you know or don't know? I don't have time for this.'

She let her gaze roam over him while he continued to loom over her. He really *did* look like he'd left wherever he had been in great haste. There was no sign of the black and gold patterned silk tie he had been wearing earlier, and his shirt was poorly tucked into the suit trousers, now badly creased, that he'd worn on the show. It didn't take a genius to guess what she'd interrupted by phoning him, and Mercy shook her head slowly.

'I never thought I'd feel sorry for Araba. And yet, the poor, deluded woman thinks you can actually remain faithful to one person. But, then again, don't they say that the way you get a man is also the way you'll lose him?'

'Leave Araba out of this,' Lucas snapped. 'You said you had something to discuss with me – no, let me get this right, you *threatened* me with something you claim you have on me. Well, I'm here now so, as I said, spit it out.'

Fed up of him towering over her, Mercy slipped off the sofa and walked a few paces away. In her bare feet, she barely reached Lucas's shoulders, but even knowing the true nature of the person she was dealing with, she strangely felt no fear. Her husband no longer had the power to intimidate her. Her eyes flicked to the photograph of a grinning Hakeem, and Lucas followed her gaze. For an instant as she stared at her beloved son her eyes misted over, and then blinking rapidly to clear her vision, she turned her attention back to the man in front of her.

'I called you because I wanted to look you in the face to tell you that you must resign as a Minister of State and do it tomorrow.'

Lucas looked incredulous. 'What the hell are you talking about?' he scoffed. 'I'm warning you, Mercy, don't play games with me.'

She nodded and walked towards the side table to pick up the blue folder, handing it to him without a word. She stepped back and watched the rush of emotions chase across his face as he flicked through the sheets. Shock, disbelief, anger, and then... naked fear. Those were the emotions she'd also experienced after stumbling across the file in his study and reading the list of names set against the sums her husband had extorted from them over the years. She remembered her disbelief at seeing the grainy but still recognisable picture of one of the country's most prominent evangelical Christians in bed with another man, and the photograph of a well-respected society matron lying naked on a bed alongside an equally well-known newspaper magnate who was not her husband. It had taken no time at all for Mercy to conclude that her husband's wealth had not been accumulated by dint of his business acumen or the hard work he frequently espoused, but had been built off the backs of rich, vulnerable people prepared to part with considerable sums of money to protect their public image.

'*How – where*—?' He paused, seemingly unable to get the words choking him out of his throat.

'That doesn't matter, Lucas. What matters is that it's over. The blackmailing, the extortion, the lies, the...' she tailed off with a sigh. 'All of it. You've fooled me for years, you're clearly fooling Araba and the Party right now, but I won't let you continue fooling this country. You have no scruples, Lucas, and God alone knows what you're capable of if you ever get your hands on the ultimate levers of power. I can't – I *won't* be an accomplice to that.'

'Don't be a fool, Mercy,' he ground out harshly. 'If I go down, you'll get dragged down with me. You've been enjoying the good life just as much as I have. And what about Hakeem? Is this what you want for our son? For his father to be disgraced – or worse? Do you realise that if these people's secrets get out and they know they have nothing left to fear from me, that you'll have signed my death warrant?'

She flinched but didn't drop her gaze. 'I'm sorry, but there's nothing I can do about that.'

'Yes, there *is*! You said it yourself. You have the power to decide whether to make all this public. As much as it hurts me to admit it, *you* have control over what happens to me now.' Without warning, the self-assurance with which Lucas had strode into the room fell away like a broken mask. His cheeks drooped and the eyes he turned upon her reminded her of a wounded puppy.

'I know I've treated you badly, Mercy, and I'm sorry.' Was that actually a tremble she could hear in his voice, Mercy wondered, bemused by the rapid unravelling of the man who had dominated her for so long. But Lucas hadn't finished. 'This thing with Araba – I'll finish it. I'll do anything you want; I *promise*!'

Mercy bit her lip as Lucas continued to plead his case, his expression imploring her to save him. When he eventually ground to a halt, she continued to watch him in silence, feeling once again the intense pain that had gripped her on the day she discovered Lucas and Araba's affair, the day when her once happy world had come to an abrupt end. Even now, she could scarcely believe how blind and gullible she had been for so long. Sweet Mercy who never questioned her good fortune or the man who had stealthily and steadily taken control of her over the years, robbing her not only of her self-confidence, but of every trace of clear-eyed common sense that might have let her see long ago who Lucas really was. *How could I have been so blind?*

'You know, I've asked myself countless times why I never saw the truth of who you really are,' Mercy said slowly. 'For years, I looked up to you as this older, mature, wise and successful man. I gave up my career and made you my life because I thought Hakeem and I came first, and that everything you did was for us. All these years when I could have achieved something for myself, and for what? To find out you're a fake, and that every lesson you've taught our son about hard work being the basis for success was a total lie.'

She glanced at Hakeem's picture and then sighed. 'Lucas, you've been a selfish and unfaithful husband but, so far at least, you've been a good father. Your son adores you and if you care anything at all about him, you'll do as I ask. Your past has finally caught up with you and the only choice you have is whether you get to control the narrative, or I give the green light to the press to run with it.'

'If you love Hakeem as much as you say you do, there's no way you'd put him through a media circus that will scar him for life,' Lucas pleaded.

Mercy bit her lip. 'But don't you see, Lucas? That's exactly what will happen if you *don't* resign. You were right about Max being up to something. He has copies of all these documents. The only reason he didn't go through with it on his show this evening was to give you a chance to step down and avoid hurting your family. If you don't, this will be the biggest scoop of his career and neither you nor I will have the power to stop him.'

Lucas shook his head violently from side to side. 'Max is in love with you. Don't look at me like that's a surprise to you! He'll do whatever you ask him to. Mercy, *please*! Do you want me to beg? Is that what you want?'

While the sight of Lucas down on his knees pleading for forgiveness would once have brought her immense satisfaction, now all Mercy felt was exhaustion from the yo-yo of emotions she'd experienced that day, and unmitigated contempt for the man standing in front of her. It was time to finish this.

'No, Lucas. I'll tell you what I want, and I warn you it's not negotiable.' She paused only briefly at the look of apprehension that descended on his face. 'I want you to step down as Minister, resign your portfolio and renounce any attempt to ever take political office in this country. I also want you to sign the divorce papers I've had drawn up and which are in that envelope on the table. They set out terms which are fair to both of us and state that I get full and sole custody of Hakeem. For our son's sake, I will never stop you from seeing him or spending time with him, but he will live with me and I will make the decisions that affect his life until he's old enough to be independent.'

Lucas looked horrified. 'You can't mean that!'

She shook her head resignedly. 'I don't even want to ask which part you're referring to, because I suspect you're more appalled by the idea of not being President than you are of losing your wife and child.'

'Mercy, be reasonable!' he blustered, a spark of his old fire returning. 'I've spent *years* building my political career. You can't just expect me to walk away—'

'Oh, but I can,' she retorted. 'Your brand of politics is fake, shallow and based on lies, and the country will manage very well without you. Look on the bright side, Lucas. You get to keep your reputation and your dignity instead of what you truly deserve. To be honest, you really don't have a choice here. If you don't agree, you'll force me to step aside and let Max throw you to the dogs. And you know what that means – public disgrace, not to mention a long prison sentence for extortion. Looking at those lists in the folder, you've successfully blackmailed a lot of powerful people and if this comes out, they'll come baying for your blood.'

It was like watching a beautiful hot air balloon deflate before her eyes. Whatever bravado had remained seeped away as Lucas slowly absorbed the words his wife spoke with unwavering conviction. Without warning, his face crumpled, and Mercy watched him stumble to the sofa and bury his head in his hands, his shoulders heaving with dry, soundless sobs.

* * *

In the end, it all happened very quickly. Two days later, as Mercy was getting ready for work, she put down her hair brush and stared at the television screen in her bedroom as the presenter breathlessly announced the breaking news that Minister of State Lucas Peterson, the man everyone had assumed would be next in line for Vice President, had suddenly resigned from the government. There had been no sightings of the former minister, and rumours were rife that he had left the country the previous evening after submitting his shock resignation to the President.

Mercy turned back to the mirror and started applying her make-up, only to swivel back to the screen at the mention of Araba's name. Having left London on an overnight flight with the other delegates on the trade mission, Araba had clearly not yet heard the news. A portly cameraman tracking her progress down the Arrivals corridor at the airport was almost running to keep up with her long strides, while a gaggle of waiting reporters lobbed questions at her. At first, Araba appeared confused by the unexpected attention and then, as the import of the journalists' questions hit her, her eyes widened, and she stopped in her tracks and covered her gasp with her hand. Recovering quickly, she pushed her way forcefully through the crowd of reporters and the people gathered around the barrier frantically trying to photograph the rumoured mistress of the minister who had disappeared into thin air.

Mercy switched off the television, unable to watch any more. Both Araba and Lucas deserved whatever was coming to them, but she had no desire to gloat. No matter what he had done, Lucas was still Hakeem's father, and she didn't want her personal feelings about her hopefully soon-to-be ex-husband to damage her son's relationship with his father. As another of her non-negotiable conditions, she and Lucas had sat down with Hakeem the previous day before Lucas had departed for the apartment in Geneva to explain to their boy that while his mother and father would no longer be a couple, he would always remain their priority. To her astonishment, after listening in silence to his parents' stumbling explanation, Hakeem had nodded sagely.

'I told Jamie you two would get divorced soon. Sorry, Mum, I might be a kid, but I'm not blind – or stupid.'

Thinking of her son brought Mercy back to earth. Glancing at the bedside clock, she quickly slipped on her shoes and reached for her handbag. The security guards would handle the pack of journalists she had no doubt would be camped on her doorstep; as far as she was concerned, both she and her child would continue life as usual – at least for now.

Walking out onto the landing, Mercy called out, '*Hakeem*! Come on, let's go or you'll be late for school. You know how bad the traffic gets if we're even a few minutes late.'

* * *

Returning to the office, Mercy turned off the radio in the car, exasperated by the fevered speculation on the part of the radio presenters, political pundits and the listeners calling in to the show about the cause of Lucas's resignation. It had been almost a week since Lucas's resignation and with no new facts emerging, some of the reasons proffered for his abrupt departure from public life were so outlandish that Mercy was beginning to question whether the truth would have been considered quite as heinous as she'd believed.

She drew up to a set of traffic lights and waited patiently while the stream of cars crossed the dual carriageway. Her mind went back to the meeting she had just concluded, and she sent up a silent prayer of thanks for Lyla. Mercy's long overdue but heartfelt apology to Theresa for her bitchiness towards her at her birthday party had restored Mercy into Lyla's good graces. So much so that her friend and neighbour had recommended a lawyer who had turned out to be every bit as approachable and professional as Lyla had promised. With Lucas agreeing to co-operate, the solicitor had assured her, Mercy stood an excellent chance of securing a speedy divorce. All being well, once the sale and division of assets and financial arrangements for Hakeem had been concluded, she could be a free woman within a matter of months.

The lights changed and Mercy shifted her car into gear and moved off, her mind still struggling to process the rapid changes taking place in her life. After more than a decade as Lucas's wife, it felt both liberating and unsettling to know she was now on her own. When Lucas had phoned from Switzerland the previous evening, Mercy had quickly passed the phone to Hakeem after only a brief greeting, feeling a deep sense of relief that she no longer needed to pretend. While she would always share a bond with Lucas because of their son, she couldn't wait to break the legal ties that shackled her to a man so lacking in principles and decency. Perhaps it was precisely because Lucas lacked any moral core that he had crumbled so quickly, Mercy pondered, as she navigated the heavy downtown traffic. The broken, subdued voice that had barely risen above a whisper when she'd answered the phone had been almost unrecognisable. Like all bullies who thrived on power and control, being stripped of both had brought Lucas face to face with his own lack of substance.

For a moment, Mercy felt a pang of regret for the old days and the old Lucas. But which Lucas had been the real one? Was it the husband whose teasing chuckle had always made her smile? The father who would tickle his son until he cried with laughter? The family man who had supported his brother's musical career and provided for his retired mother? Or was it the ruthless, ambitious man who had extorted and terrorised people to build a fortune? The deceitful spouse who had cared so little for his marriage and so much for gaining power that starting a relationship with his wife's best friend had never posed a problem? If he hadn't suffered before, Mercy acknowledged, exiled from the country he had come so close to leading, Lucas was certainly suffering now.

With the mask of power and prestige torn away, the broken man inside had been left with nowhere to hide. While he had escaped jail, having been stripped of his political influence and the adulation he craved, Lucas would never escape the punishment that would hurt him the most. Without question, the worst sentence a man like Lucas could ever envisage was knowing he had been so close to the ultimate seat of power and seeing that victory snatched from him.

Turning into the broad tree-lined avenue leading to Bamford Media's office, Mercy took several deep breaths, slowly releasing the air from her lungs and letting the tension that had built up over the past few days flow gently from her body. It was all over now, and the years of misery would soon be consigned to history. It was time to focus on building a new life for herself and for her beloved Hakeem.

The security guard standing at the entrance to the office raised the gates and Mercy drove into the grounds and circled the car park, quickly finding a space under the shade of a spreading acacia tree. She reached for her bag and stepped out of the car into the sunshine, her thoughts already shifting to the script she needed to complete for Max's new documentary. Smiling happily, and with a spring in her step, she hurried inside the building and towards her future.

Epilogue

With most of the furniture now sold or packed into storage, the big house felt enormous. Mercy wandered out of the living room and into the space which had until the previous week been occupied by the huge ebony dining table that had easily sat twenty people.

She had lived in the house for years, and yet Mercy felt like a stranger as she left the dining room to cross the hallway into the room which had once been Lucas's study and was now empty of all furnishings except the bookcases the new owners had asked to keep. She couldn't wait for the weekend when she and Hakeem would move into the modest three-bedroom house she had signed the lease for only a fortnight earlier.

As part of the divorce agreement, the Marula Heights mansion had been put up for sale, and by the coming Sunday Mercy, Hakeem, and the ever loyal Esi, would be living close to Stella's modest housing development and a short drive from Hakeem's school.

After almost a year abroad, Lucas had returned to Ghana for a brief visit, keeping a low profile as he quietly wound down the bulk of his business interests in the country. Following the government's controversial decision to renegotiate almost all its treaty arrangements with its key trading partners, Araba was frequently featured on the news. Mercy had no idea if she and Lucas were still an item as she restricted all communication with her ex-husband to matters relating to their son. But, knowing Araba's penchant for power, Mercy suspected that Lucas's fall from grace would have put paid to their relationship. The President's fury at the persistent rumours that the Party had somehow engineered his prized minister's sudden resignation, had further exacerbated Lucas's status of persona non grata within the ruling party. Given that both Araba and Lucas had shown such remarkable similarity in treating relationships as a transaction, and knowing her ex-husband's track record with women, Mercy strongly doubted that Lucas would concern himself with Araba now he was out of the Party.

She looked at her watch and squealed in horror at the time. Dashing up the stairs, she stripped off her T-shirt and jeans and tossed them on her bed before racing into the bathroom for a speedy shower. Emerging from the bathroom, she moisturised her skin carefully and slipped into the lacy new underwear she had been saving for weeks. Sliding open her wardrobe, she pulled out a short, black dress and stepped into it carefully, letting the soft material slide up over her curvy hips and small waist. She moved over to stand in front of the full-length mirror on the wall and her big brown eyes twinkled back at her as she smiled mischievously at her reflection. Her gaze dropped to examine the plunging neckline enhanced by the clinging fabric. Was this the right look for her first date as a newly single woman? Mercy's smile widened. *I'll soon find out.*

When the doorbell rang half an hour later, Mercy felt a shiver of nerves run through her. With Hakeem staying over at his grandmother's, and Esi off for the night, Mercy was the only one available to answer the door. Taking a deep breath, she smoothed down her dress and hurried to open the front door.

'Max!'

With a grin that matched her own, Max thrust the huge bouquet of flowers he was holding in her direction. 'Why do you look so surprised – weren't you expecting me?'

'Stop teasing and come inside. Oh, Max, these flowers are beautiful!'

She stood back for him to enter and closed the door behind him. With a squeal of excitement, Mercy brought the flowers up to her face and breathed in their fragrance.

She smiled at him happily and reached up to kiss his cheek.

'Thank you so much – they're gorgeous. Honestly, Max, you're so *sweet*...' she tailed off and looked up again.

Max raised a quizzical eyebrow at her sheepish expression, and then as he took in the significance of her words, his lips twitched.

They stared at each other in silence, and then burst into laughter.

The End

If you enjoyed reading *Sweet Mercy,* please take a moment to write a review on Amazon, Goodreads, BookBub, or any other platforms you use.

Even if it's only a line or two, I'd really appreciate it!

Also in the Marula Heights series:

RIVER WILD

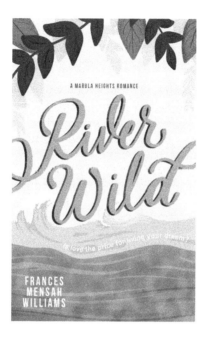

Is love the price for living your dream?

Ambitious real estate agent River Osei loves her job and dreams of living in a home as beautiful as those she sells to her clients. Putting marriage to her artist boyfriend Cameron on the back burner, River's only focus is to hit her house fund target.

But River's plan is thrown into turmoil when she negotiates a sale to demanding music mogul, Donald Ayo. He is immediately taken with her, and she is equally taken with his house – a beautiful mansion in the luxurious gated community of Marula Heights. With Donald pressing for a deal that includes more than a house, River is forced to choose between the man she loves and a lifestyle she craves.

But living the dream isn't always what it seems and even the best fantasies come at a cost. Faced with the real-life consequences of her choice, River must learn that a house is not a home and love is not for sale.

Available now on Amazon and online retailers in eBook and paperback.

* * *

Praise for *River Wild*

'This is a great book and as always the author brings her characters to life so well. It was a joy to read.'

'Kept me captivated and guessing throughout.'
Amazon reviewers

Sweet Mercy is a companion story to

IMPERFECT ARRANGEMENTS

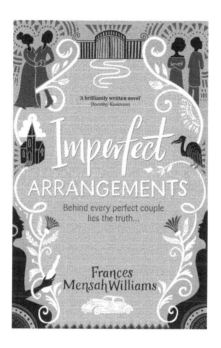

There are two sides to every story...

In the sun-soaked capital of Ghana, best friends Theresa, Maku and Lyla struggle with the arrangements that define their relationships.

Ambitious, single-minded Theresa has gambled everything to move with her loving husband Tyler from London to cosmopolitan Accra. But when shocking developments threaten their plans, they also expose the hidden cracks in their fairytale marriage.

Feisty Maku is desperate for professional recognition – and her dream white wedding. But how long can she wait for her laid-back partner Nortey to stop dreaming up pointless projects from the comfort of his local bar and stand up to his family?

Churchgoing Lyla married Kwesi in haste, and six years later she is desperate for a child. But while she battles a vicious mother-in-law, and her growing attraction to the mysterious Reuben, her husband has bitten off more than he can chew with his latest mistress.

Facing lies, betrayal, and shattered illusions, each couple must confront the truth of who they have become and the arrangements they have enabled. Against the backdrop of a shifting culture, each woman must decide what – and who – she is willing to sacrifice for the perfect marriage.

Available on Amazon and online retailers and from selected booksellers.

Praise for *Imperfect Arrangements*

'The queen of romantic dramas is back... this charming read is about the challenges which come with friendship, love, and relationships, and the search for that happily ever after.'
The Top 20 African Books of 2020, African Arguments

'Following three couples on the cusp of significant life changes, this charming romance... explores the difficulties of relationships at varying stages. Williams... weaves in vivid cultural details as she lifts the veil on the realities of marriage, the woes of infertility, and the strain of gender roles. Readers are sure to enjoy this uplifting work.'
Publishers Weekly

'The beautiful, tropical backdrop is the ideal setting for this tale that is crammed with realistic, complex characters. It is an easy-to-read exploration of modern love and relationships. I very much enjoyed this brilliantly written novel.'
Dorothy Koomson, bestselling author of *The Ice Cream Girls* and *Tell Me Your Secret*

'In *Imperfect Arrangements*, Frances Mensah Williams slices through the lives of three couples and presents a witty, true, and, sometimes, heartbreaking portrayal of married life in Accra, Ghana.'
Ayesha Harruna Attah, author of *Harmattan Rain* and *The Hundred Wells of Salaga*

'This novel is a celebration of sisterhood. You'll cheer on Theresa, Lyla and Maku as they navigate life in modern Accra, dealing with difficult bosses, feckless husbands and dubious mother-in-laws. You won't want to put the story down till it ends.'
Chibundu Onuzo, author of *The Spider King's Daughter* and *Welcome to Lagos*

**For more about Frances Mensah Williams
and her books:**

Visit my website at www.francesmensahwilliams.com

Connect with me
Twitter: @FrancesMensahW
Facebook: www.facebook.com/francesmensahwilliams
Instagram: francesmensahw

Other Books
by Frances Mensah Williams

Fiction

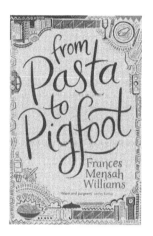

From Pasta to Pigfoot

On a mission to find love, a disastrous night out leaves pasta-fanatic Faye's romantic dreams in tatters and underscores her alienation from her African heritage. Leaving London to find out what she's missing, Faye is whisked into the hectic social whirlpool of Ghana and into a world of food, fun and sun to face choices she had never thought possible.

From Pasta to Pigfoot: Second Helpings

Pasta fanatic Faye Bonsu seems to have it all; a drop-dead gorgeous boyfriend, a bourgeoning new career and a rent-free mansion to call home. But with friends shifting into yummy mummy mode, a man with no desire to put a ring on it, tricky clients, and an attractive and very single boss, things are not exactly straightforward. Faye returns to sunny Ghana, but life doesn't always offer second chances.

Non-Fiction

I Want to Work in Africa: How to Move Your Career to the World's Most Exciting Continent

A practical, invaluable guide to the African job market, the industries and professions in demand, how to put in place a winning strategy, write a compelling CV, make the right connections, and find a job in Africa that builds on your career and talents. Illustrated with personal stories and full of practical advice from recruiters and professionals who work in Africa.

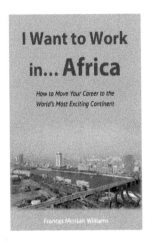

Everyday Heroes: Learning from the Careers of Successful Black Professionals

A collection of interviews with sixteen professionals with different careers including law, accountancy, music, publishing, medicine, banking and architecture. These 'everyday heroes' talk about what it takes to succeed in their careers, their own influences and the life lessons they have learned along the way.

Lightning Source UK Ltd.
Milton Keynes UK
UKHW010629080421
381648UK00001B/199

9 780956 917584